Wild Bride

~ West Series ~
Billy & Savannah
© 2014 Jill Sanders

Follow Jill online at:
Jill@JillSanders.com
http://JillSanders.com
Jill on Twitter
Jill on Facebook
Sign up for Jill's Newsletter

Summary

Spoiled rich girl Savannah has always had a lust for sexy men, a wild appetite for partying, and a blatant disregard for others. When she finds herself pregnant and alone after burning all her bridges, it looks like she'll be getting a taste of her own medicine. Stubborn and set in her ways, she pushes away the only person who really cares.

Billy has one goal—to convince Savannah that hope and happiness are still within reach. But something's got to give.

Wild Bride

by

Jill Sanders

Jill Sanders

4

Prologue

Savannah lay very still. Her small six-year-old heart beat way too fast in her chest, causing her head to hurt. Even with her eyes squeezed tightly shut, she knew that he stood over her.

She'd known he would come to her when she saw her parents drive away just before her bedtime. Her hands shook as the covers were pulled away from her little body. She didn't cry out until his large hands reached around her tiny neck and squeezed. Then she retreated deep into her mind and everything went dark.

When she awoke again, it was to screaming. Her mother stood over her and cried out as her father rushed into the room.

"Mama?" she croaked out. Her throat hurt and when she tried to move, her little body screamed out in pain.

"Hush now." Her mother came rushing to her side. "Don't move, sweet baby."

It was then that she glanced over at her father's face. She'd never seen him look like he did now. When his eyes met hers, he blinked a few times and then turned and rushed from the room.

Her mother had gathered her up in her arms and was rubbing her long blonde hair, soothing all the aches and pains in her body. She cried in her mother's arms until she fell back to sleep.

When she woke this time, the lights were bright in her eyes and she closed them again tightly. When someone's hands touched her arm, she jolted and kicked out, screaming, "No!"

"It's okay, baby," her mother said right next to her. She opened her eyes and found her mother's face. "The doctor just wants a look at you." Her mother smiled and rubbed her hair again. "He won't hurt you."

Savannah looked over to an older gentlemen she'd known her entire life. Dr. Williams had been her doctor for as long as she could remember. She dropped her arms and nodded, seeing the doctor smile down at her.

Then he leaned back and nodded to her mother. Her mother frowned and hugged her tighter.

"I think Savannah would like a warm bath now," the doctor said as he smiled down at her and patted her hand. "Ruth, why don't you take her in and help her."

When her mother lifted her from her bed, she cried out a little as her body shifted. "I'm sorry, baby," her mother whispered, burying her face in her hair.

As they walked past her father, she noticed his face again. This time there were dark bruises on his left cheek, his nose looked a little off, and there was blood dripping from a small cut just below his left cheek.

"Pa?" She reached out for him as her mother carried her past.

"It's okay, baby. I'll be right here when you get done with your bath." Her father kissed her forehead.

When her mother finally sat her in the warm bubble bath, she lay back and closed her eyes. "Am I going to school today?"

Her mother's hand stilled from running the soft washcloth over her shoulders. "No, baby." She watched as a tear escaped her mother's eye. "No, baby, you don't have to do anything you don't want to do ever again."

Jill Sanders

Chapter One

Ten years later...

Those words had stuck in Savannah's mind, and she had lived by them. It had cost her a few close childhood friends, but others had stood by her. Others who not only looked up to her but almost worshiped her.

It was her sixteenth birthday and tonight was going to be the biggest and best party the small town of Fairplay had ever seen.

Shortly after that evil night, her father had signed the paperwork that had forever changed their lives. Now the Douglases were rolling in money, allowing them to afford the biggest house for hundreds of miles and the best clothes they could buy in the city. Everyone in town respected them and gave them anything they wanted.

She smiled as she applied a little more makeup to her eyes. The reflection looking back at her was almost perfect. Picking up the tube of lip gloss, she applied the red color heavily on her lips and smiled. There.

Her new cream-colored blouse, which she'd bought the last time her mother had driven her to Houston, looked perfect. She'd gained ample cleavage earlier than most of the other schoolgirls. She frowned a little when she looked down at her large chest. Actually, she was still growing. The last trip into the city, she'd had to go up a whole bra size.

She looked at her reflection again and smiled. The boys in town, especially the cute ones, always stared at her chest. Her long blonde hair, her perfect features, and her toned body also got attention, but nothing made the boys come running like when she showed off her chest in tight clothes.

Standing up, she looked at her reflection in the full-length mirror in the corner of her large room. The dark blue silk skirt flowed when she walked towards the mirror, and she watched how her feet looked in the heels she'd bought. She'd spent more money than her mother had wanted on them, but they were perfect for her outfit, and they made her feet look smaller somehow.

Turning, she watched as her short skirt lifted, showing off part of her upper thighs. She'd worked hard in gym class to make sure she stayed in shape. Even though her teacher was a complete idiot and hardly ever had the class do squats, she could see the slight difference in her legs since she'd been doing them at home the last few months.

"Savannah?" her mother called from downstairs.

"I'll be down in a minute," she called back and rushed over to grab her new fur coat. Even though it was in the high seventies tonight, she pulled on the white softness and smiled again and then sprayed herself with her new expensive perfume. Tonight, everyone would be looking at her, and she wanted to be perfect. This was her night. Grabbing her clutch purse, she took one last look in the mirror and smiled.

When she walked down the stairs, trailing her manicured fingertips down the smooth wood, she smiled at her parents who stood at the bottom. Her mother wore a long green dress that she'd helped pick out just for the occasion. Her father looked as handsome as ever in his suit and tie. She didn't see the lines on their faces or the fact that her father's hair was starting to go gray. She could only see the love that these two people had given her.

"You look wonderful," her mother said, smiling.

She could see a slight tear in her father's eyes as he looked at her. "I can't believe my little girl is sixteen."

When she stood at the bottom of the stairs, she reached up to kiss them both.

Her father took her shoulders. "Before you head

into town for your party, we wanted to give you our gift." He smiled and kept holding her.

"Well?" She frowned a little when he didn't move, so she held out her hands.

He chuckled. She'd always loved the sound of her father's laughter and smiled back.

"Daddy, where's my gift?" She stomped her foot lightly and smiled.

"In just a minute." He glanced down at her again and leaned down to hug her once more. Then he turned and took her mother's hand and walked towards the front door.

"We hope you like it," her mother said as they opened the front door.

Outside, in their circle driveway, sat a brand new car. She squealed and rushed from the house.

"It's the newest BMW. I hope you like it." Her father held up the keys.

Savannah didn't care what kind of car it was— it was red and a convertible. She was going to be the most popular girl in school when everyone saw her drive into the school parking lot in this.

"Can I drive it into town for my party?" She took the keys from her father. He smiled and nodded. Then she hugged them both and jumped into her very first car as they watched. "We'll be right behind you," he said.

She loved the smell of the new car. The leather

interior felt warm and rich next to her skin. She set her small silk purse down in the seat next to her and put the key in the ignition. She'd gotten her license a few days earlier on her actual birthday, and she'd driven alone a few times this last week. But this was *her* car and she was heading to *her* party. She wanted this moment to last forever.

"We'll see you in town." Her father leaned in the door and kissed her cheek. "Drive safe."

"I always do, Daddy." She waved at her mother and shut the door. When she turned the key, the car turned on and she felt a wave of excitement rush through her.

She was telling the truth. She did always drive carefully. Just last year, several high school seniors had been involved in a crash. They'd been racing another car full of teens and had lost control of the truck. Everyone in school had heard the horror stories of how the paramedics had had to scrape several of them off the cement. No, Savannah wasn't going to end up like that.

She gripped the wheel tighter and made sure to take the turn out of her driveway slowly. It took only a few minutes to get into town.

Fairplay, Texas, had always been home. Even though it was a small and somewhat boring town, she still loved it. She asked to be taken into Houston or Dallas for all her shopping, but living in a small town like Fairplay did have its advantages. For one, her family was the wealthiest in town, thanks to the deal her parents had made with the oil companies. That made her the best-dressed and most envied girl in town. She had more friends and more male admirers than anyone else in school.

When she parked outside of the large town hall building, she couldn't help but feel excited. There were hundreds of cars parked outside and it took her a few minutes to find the perfect parking spot for her new car. She could hear the music pumping from inside and almost jumped out of the car, forgetting her purse.

Leaning in, she grabbed it off the seat just as she felt a wave of fear jump over her skin. She jolted up and turned around quickly to see a man standing a few feet away. The dark parking lot shadowed his face, but she knew instantly who it was.

"What do you want?" she almost screamed.

"Well, well. Look who's all grown up." He took a few steps closer to her, his eyes running over her top, which was exposed since her fur coat was open to the evening air. She quickly pulled it closed, hiding her large chest from his eyes. "Heard you were having a party. Thought I'd come and give my dear niece a present." She felt a shiver run down her body at the word. "Especially now that she's become a woman." He smiled and stopped less than a foot from her.

Savannah's back was up against her new car.

The door was still open and just the smell of her uncle mixed with the new car smell soiled the wonderful scent for her, causing her stomach to turn even more.

"You're not invited," she said softly, putting her purse between them and holding her fur coat closed tightly. She felt herself shiver and hated that she was losing control.

She watched in disgust as his eyes raked over her. Her uncle Joe was nothing like her father. Even though they were brothers, Joe's life had taken a turn for the worse early on in life. Or so her father had told her.

In the last ten years, Joe had been in and out of prison more times than she cared to count. And most of it was thanks to her.

"If you don't leave, I'll call the cops." She tried to push her chin up. She was almost as tall as him now and yet he still made her feel like she was six years old.

His eyes darkened. "Call them. I ain't doin' nothing wrong."

She frowned and whispered. "You're alive."

His eyes grew dark and just as his hands reached out to grab her, a car's high beams hit them. She heard tires squeal as her parent's truck stopped a few feet from them.

Then her father was pulling Joe away from her, and she watched in horror as her father's fists

15

slammed her uncle in the face repeatedly.

Her mother rushed to her side and pulled her towards their truck.

"Are you okay? Did he touch you?" her mother asked over and over.

"I'm okay," she said, not realizing she was shaking. "Mom." She stopped her mother when she realized she was trying to push her into the truck. "Stop daddy. He's going to kill him." She nodded towards her father who was sitting on top of Joe, still pumping his fists into his face.

"I've called Stephen," she said, absentmindedly.

Stephen Miller was the sheriff of Fairplay and the only person in town, besides her parents, who knew what had happened to her all those years ago.

She nodded and got into the truck and watched as her mother rushed over to her father and pulled on his arm until he stopped punching his now-unconscious brother.

Her parents stood over the man until the sheriff's car drove up.

When Sheriff Miller walked over to her, after loading her uncle into the back of his car, she answered his questions and avoided looking at him.

"Well, it would sure be a shame for you to miss your own party." He looked around and she realized her eyes were wet and quickly dashed away the tears. "I don't think anyone saw this mess." He put a hand on hers and waited until she looked up at him. "Why don't you freshen up and go have a good time. I know for a fact that every high school student in town is in the hall, waiting to wish you a happy birthday."

She nodded and when he stepped away, her mother got closer. "If you would rather—"

"No." She straightened her shoulders. This was her night. She wasn't going to let anything or anyone take this away from her. She was Savannah Douglas, the most popular girl in school. She was going to clean up her face and walk into her sixteenth birthday party and have the time of her life.

Ten minutes later, she opened the outer doors to the hall, took a deep breath, and swore that no one would ever make her feel that way again. She would be the strongest person she could be and never let anyone see weakness in her ever again. She hated that a man could make her feel small, like she wasn't in control.

When she stepped in, the music stopped and "Happy Birthday" started playing. Spotlights hit her face and she smiled and played the part of Savannah Douglas for the whole town to see. She hid her fears and insecurities so well from everyone that night that no one suspected anything.

After dancing with every boy that had been

invited and chatting with and hugging every girl, she opened presents and blew out her candles while every eye was on her. She laughed, gossiped, and flirted until she felt her energy start to drain.

Then she pulled Travis, a boy whose attentions she'd been dying to have, into a dark corner and made out with him. She pulled him closer and whispered for him to take her somewhere private. Travis was in the same grade as her, and he was the star in almost every school sport. His father was the mayor of Fairplay and probably would be until he died.

Travis was tall and good looking, and she'd determined that she would allow him to be her first. She knew it wasn't really her first time, but she was going to take control and force her mind to clear the past, making this her true first.

"Heard you got a new car." He smiled down at her. "What are the chances of you letting me drive her?" he asked as they walked out the back door and headed towards the parking lot.

He lit up a cigarette and handed it to her. She'd never tried smoking, but she took the cigarette and took a deep puff, enjoying the richness of it. She wanted more than anything to leave her childhood behind her tonight, so she didn't mind the sting in her throat or the fact that her lungs hurt and she felt like coughing. She sucked in another puff and followed him across the parking lot.

She thought about the mixture of new car smell

and her uncle and shivered. "Sure, why not." She handed him the keys and held onto his hand as they walked towards her car.

When she sat in the passenger seat, she forced every ounce of fear out of her mind and only focused on where she was, who she was with. She was determined to make the most of her life and that meant getting over her childhood fears.

Her uncle was right in one way. She was a woman now. And she was more determined than ever to never show weakness. After all, her party had been a huge success and she'd eaten up all the attention she'd gotten. She'd loved every jealous look from all the girls and every lusty glance from all the boys and was determined to continue getting every ounce of attention she could.

She didn't mind so much that some friends had stepped away from her; you couldn't please everyone. She smiled as Travis drove to the local make out spot and parked.

Yes, tonight she would become a full woman. A woman who was one hundred percent in control of her own life. And she was going to do everything in her power to make sure she never lost that control again.

Chapter Two

Ten years later...

Her life was over. She frowned as she looked at the full-length mirror that still stood in the same spot in the corner of her room. Even though the furniture had changed a little, it was still her childhood room. She'd changed styles and had had the room painted and decorated so many times she couldn't remember most of the styles, but one thing was still clear. This was still her space.

She closed her eyes and wished more than anything that she hadn't been the one to wreck her life. It was her scheming that had backfired. She hadn't seen this coming at all.

She frowned and thought of Billy. Closing her eyes, she tried to get his face out of her mind. Reaching for her cigarettes, she closed her fingers over the pack and gasped. Her hand moved away from the desired package. Her eyes moved to the full-length mirror again and she sat down on the edge of her bed. She felt like crying. Her life was over. She repeated it over and over in her mind.

Everything she'd worked so hard for in the last ten years was gone. Here she was in her mid-twenties and she'd screwed everything up herself.

She had no real education. No job. Nothing. Leaning back on her bed, she sighed and wished for a do-over. Just one night. Less than a month ago, on a cool spring night.

Just then, her cell rang. Reaching over without opening her eyes, she answered it.

"Hey, are you going to tell me?" He sounded worried.

"Yes," she whispered.

"Yes, you're going to tell me? Or yes, yes?"

"Yes," she repeated.

The line was quiet. "I'm coming over," he said quickly.

"No." She opened her eyes and sat up.

"Why?"

"I..." She had no real excuses to give.

"I'll be there in ten minutes," he said and hung up.

What had she done? She looked down at her new iPhone and felt like throwing it. What *had* she done? She set her phone down and closed her eyes again and felt a wave of sickness rush through her. When she opened her eyes again, she felt the room spin and had to rush to her bathroom and get sick.

By the time she'd cleaned up, she heard a light tap on her bedroom window and walked over to let Billy in.

It wasn't as if she didn't like him. After all, Billy had been one of the best-looking guys in school. But they'd been out of school for years now, and Billy was like a lot of guys who had stayed in town after school. He worked a dead-end job, drank too much, and ran around with any available girls that weren't married off.

How had she ever gotten together with him?

She watched him step into her room and sighed. He was impressive. Even though he was a screw up, he was easily better looking than any other man in Fairplay.

His dark hair was a little longer and pushed back away from his chiseled face. His dark eyes were easily one of his best features. His nose was straight and led your eyes down to the perfect lips that had somehow escaped her attention for so many years.

"So," he said, shoving his hands into his worn jeans and looking at her.

"So." She walked over and sat on her bed.

"Are you okay?" He sat next to her.

"Yeah." She looked down as his hands took hers.

"I…" he started. She looked up at him. "I didn't mean for this…"

She chuckled. "Yeah, neither did I."

"Well, since it did…" She watched him swallow. "Will you marry me?"

She couldn't stop the burst of laughter that had built up in her chest. "Hell, no." She stood up and turned on him. "Seriously? Why would I follow up a stupid mistake with an even bigger one?" She turned and started listing off all the reasons it was a very bad idea. By the time she'd run out of steam, he was nodding and slowly getting off her bed.

"Well, if you need anything." He avoided looking at her, and she knew that she'd hurt him. At this point, she didn't care.

There was no way she was going to marry Billy Jackson, even if she was having his baby.

Six months later…

Shortly after that night, she'd traveled to Vegas after finding out from Billy that Travis, Billy's longtime best friend, was there. She'd hoped to try and convince him to come back into town, to help her make things right, but instead he'd shunned her and she'd returned home empty-handed and empty-hearted. Not that she was in love with Travis Nolan. But he was the one person throughout all the years who had always been there when she needed someone. Even when he was engaged to wiry Alexis West, he'd been there for her. She'd loved knowing that she'd been with Travis the entire time he'd been roping Alex along. But after his mother had gone crazy, Travis had left town. She hadn't seen again until Vegas.

Now, there was no hiding the fact that she was pregnant anymore. Even her parents knew, though they had never actually asked outright.

She'd stopped smoking and only occasionally walked around with a lite cigarette hanging from her mouth, just to keep gossip down to a minimum. She'd even pretended to drink beer and act a little drunk in front of her friends.

Travis had come back into town and just the other night she'd made a fool out of herself on his front porch. She knew she was being childish, but it had stung that he'd turned her away so easily.

That night, she'd stood in front of the mirror naked and had lost it. Her body was a mess. So, she'd done the only thing she could think of— she'd dressed as sexy as she could and thrown herself at what she had assumed was a sure thing, only to be thrown out like a used tissue. She'd said and done some things in the last few months that she wasn't too proud of, but she had no control over herself when it came to rejection.

She hated knowing that Travis had moved on with the bookworm, Holly Bridles, who had broken Savannah's nose a few months back. Her mother had driven her into Houston and they'd preformed a minor surgery to fix it as best as they could. Still, she thought that after the baby was born, she'd fly to LA and have a professional do a better job on it.

To be honest with herself, at this point in her life, she doubted she could deal with Travis anymore. His father had just passed away and left him with a mess around town. Everyone was talking about all hoops he had to jump through just to get his hands on his family's money. She sighed and leaned back in the seat of her Jeep.

She knew the gossip that was going around town about her and Travis. Some claimed it was his baby, and she'd let the gossip continue unchecked, if for no reason other than she just didn't have the strength to fight against a whole town at this point.

Okay, it might also have been that she didn't want people to know it was Billy's child. After all, since that night when he'd found out, he'd done little to prove to her that he was going to be a man and step up, other than throwing out a hasty proposal. He'd been seen around town with his friend Corey, chasing after every available girl above the age of eighteen.

She sighed and wished more than anything that

she lived in a city instead of a small town that had nothing better to do than gossip about her life.

She jumped when she heard a knock on her window. Looking out, she saw Sheriff Miller standing next to her Jeep on the curb. Rolling down the window, she smiled at him.

"Everything okay, Savannah?" He leaned on her door and watched her carefully.

"Yeah, just resting my eyes for a moment." She smiled and put her hand over his.

"We're all worried about you, you know."

"Yeah." She frowned a little and looked down at their hands. Stephen Miller was the only man in town besides her father that she could trust. "I'm okay, really."

"If you ever need anything…" He nodded to her growing belly and trailed off.

She placed a hand over her belly and nodded. "We'll be okay. I promise."

He smiled and then tipped his hat. "Well, you keep us posted. I know you and Jamella have had words in the past, but she's really concerned for you as well."

She didn't doubt him. She had never really gotten along with the large black woman who ran Mama's diner (but seemed to think she ran the tiny town), but she respected her. You'd have to be

27

stupid not to. After all, the woman weighed more than most people in town and knew everyone else's business. With that much power, people tended to steer clear of her bad side.

"Thanks."

"Well, night." He tipped his hat again.

"Night." She reached over and started the Jeep's engine.

As she drove through town, she thought about her options.

She could move to Tyler and have the baby there. She could get an apartment and live comfortably enough. If anyone asked, she could tell them that the daddy had died overseas in the military or some other fancy tale that would explain the lack of a man in her life. She frowned at that thought.

Or she could give the baby up for adoption. She shivered and closed her mind to that. Her parents wouldn't like that either. Her mother was acting so excited about the possibility of having the baby around. She'd even gone to her last two doctor appointments with her.

Or she could have the baby and hold her head up high and raise it alone. After all, it was the twenty-first century. Women did it all the time.

She smiled. That was the plan she was most sure about. She had her parents to help out. How bad could it be raising a child alone? She could just imagine it. Her mother would take care of the baby when she wanted to go out with friends. Her dad would spoil the baby and throw big parties for it. She laughed remembering how her father had spoiled her and imagined he'd do the same for her baby.

She stopped smiling when she drove up to the house and saw Billy's truck parked out front, right by her parents' vehicles.

Billy sat on the Douglas's sofa feeling very uncomfortable. He'd taken Travis's advice to come over, but the second he'd stepped inside their door, he'd wished he hadn't.

Travis had been his best friend since grade school and he'd always looked up to him. But at this moment, he wished he was punching the man in his face rather than sitting on an uncomfortable sofa as two of the wealthiest people in town stared him down.

He knew what they saw. He was in his late twenties. Thanks to the fight he'd gotten in with Travis the other night, he was sporting a black eye and fat lip. But, he had to admit, getting punched had knocked some sense into him.

He'd been acting like a child ever since

Savannah had said all those things to him a few months ago. He'd been very hurt that she'd shunned him.

He couldn't blame her. His family members weren't exactly known for their good citizenship. After all, his father was serving time in prison for killing a man. Billy's mind flashed to the scene just a few nights ago when he'd shown up drunk at Travis' door.

"I don't need your help. I don't need anyone's help. You think I haven't heard what everyone's saying about me? That Billy Jackson, he'll end up killing himself or someone else. That Billy Jackson won't amount to anything. He'll turn out just like his old man."

"Billy, everyone can change. Look at me." Travis said, looking down at his feet. *"Look at my family. Does that mean I'll end up like my mother?"*

Billy stopped and looked at him, then shook his head no. "You're nothing like your old lady." It was true; everyone in town knew it. Travis Nolan was not crazy.

"Why don't you come in and sleep it off. I've got some of Jamella's apple pie left in the fridge.

"Really?" Billy looked off towards the house. "What about her?" He nodded towards the garage, where Travis' new fling stood on the

stairs.

"She's staying at the apartment. I'm in the big house for now." His friend's words had shocked him. After all, just a few weeks ago, he and Corey had done a number on Travis' old apartment, just to show him what they thought of how he was treating them.

"Oh, shit. Really?" Billy looked towards the garage and back towards him feeling like a heel.

"Billy?" Travis took a step towards him.

"We thought. That is…Savannah said…" He remembered the night he'd called her and she'd been crying. She'd claimed that Travis had said all sorts of things about him and Corey.

"What did you do?" He took his friend's arm.

"Shit." Billy yanked his arm away.

"It was you, wasn't it? You broke into the apartment and destroyed Holly's stuff," he asked.

"We didn't break in. We still had the key you gave us. Besides, it was all Savannah's idea. She's the one that said you'd tossed her out and was shacking up with the book woman." He had nodded towards Holly. It had hurt that Savannah had wanted Travis more than him. That knowledge alone had driven him to destroy most of Travis' stuff.

"Why?" It was Holly that asked from just behind him. "Why did you trash it?"

31

"We thought Travis was staying there." He frowned down at his fists and realized he hurt more about Savannah's decision to pick Travis over him than he did about anything Travis had done.

"I heard. Why did you break in and ruin what you thought was your friend's stuff?"

Billy shrugged his shoulders and looked down at his feet. "It seemed the thing to do after Travis started acting like we were scum." He didn't want to admit the truth.

"What?" Travis asked, stepping closer. "I never treated you like you were scum."

"Sure you did. You wouldn't hang out with us. And every time you saw us, you had this funny look on your face like you smelled something bad."

"I didn't mean to treat you bad. It's hard for me." He dropped his hands. "I don't want to go back to being bad boy Travis Nolan."

Billy laughed. "You'll always be bad boy Travis Nolan. You're the one that taught us how to shoot, how to smoke. You gave me my first beer." He shook his head. "Hell, the whole town saw your ass when we streaked during the homecoming game our senior year." Billy laughed, remembering.

Travis laughed and slapped his friend on the shoulder. "Good ol' times." Then he sobered. "But

32

for me they have to be in the past. I don't want to be the same kid I used to be."

Billy looked down at his feet. The word kid rang over and over in his head. "Hell, I know I have to shape up." He looked up at Travis and decided it was now or never. He had to tell someone. "I've got my own kid on the way in the next few weeks."

"What?" Travis looked at him and smiled. "Well, hell. I didn't know you'd shacked up with someone special."

Billy looked down again. "I meant to tell you." Then he glanced up and felt his fingers tingle as he said the next words. "Course she's telling everyone in town the baby is yours."

He watched as acknowledgment crossed Travis' eyes, and then his friend gasped. "Savannah? Savannah's baby?"

Billy smiled and nodded as he held his breath. "I know you two used to have a thing. But, well, after you left town, we sorta hooked up."

Travis laughed. "Of course you did."

Well, of course he'd gone and listened to his friend's advice. The last few days he'd spent almost every night over at Travis' house, hanging out with him, talking. It had surprised him how much Travis had gone through in the last few years since leaving Fairplay.

Because of his friend, he'd stopped drinking and had even started wearing a nicotine patch so he could stop smoking. It was making him a little jittery, but so far he was sticking it out.

Now he wished more than anything for a cigarette as he felt Savannah's parents watching him.

"So, do you mind telling us what this is all about?" Savannah's father asked, leaning forward in the chair.

"No, sir. I think it's best to wait for Savannah." He swallowed and wished she'd hurry up and get home. He knew that she had no idea he was coming out here tonight; it was one of the reasons he had come. If she'd known, she would have talked him out of it. She had a way of convincing him to do just what she wanted. Well, that was going to stop. The first step towards becoming a man was to own up to his mistakes.

He felt relief flood him when he finally heard the front door open. Then she walked in and he felt nervous all over again.

She was still as beautiful as ever. Even with the extra weight and the large belly protruding out in front of her. He didn't know her exact due date, since she hadn't shared that knowledge with him, but she was bound to be due any day now.

He stood up and walked towards her.

"Billy." He could hear the stress in her voice

and when he took her hand, she yanked it away. "What on earth are you doing here?" she whispered.

"I'm here to set things right." He took her hand again and held it tight. Then he turned to her parents. "Mr. and Mrs. Douglas, I've tried to make things right with your daughter, but I've come over here tonight for one last chance. I'm the father of Savannah's baby." He watched Mr. Douglas's eyes heat. He glanced over to Savannah's mother and saw her eyes soften. "I've asked Savannah for her hand, but she's denied me." He glanced over at Savannah and saw her eyes heat and felt her hand jump in his. "Since she won't have me, I have an alternative plan."

Mr. Douglas stood, his fists by his side. "I'm listening."

"John." Mrs. Douglas stood and put her hand on her husband's arm. "Why don't we all sit down and listen to what William has to say."

It was one of the first times anyone had ever called him by his full name, and he respected Savannah's mother even more for giving him the chance.

Savannah's father nodded and relaxed his fists as he sat back down.

"Daddy," Savannah started to say, but she stopped when her father shook his head no.

"We'll listen to what William has to say. After

all, you've made it very clear that you're not in your right mind at the moment." Her father frowned and motioned for them to sit back down.

He tugged on Savannah's hand until she followed him to the sofa where he helped her sit down.

She was a lot larger than he'd thought and when he sat next to her, he felt concerned that she was uncomfortable. She glared at him and he realized then that she wanted to kill him. He almost chuckled.

"I know Savannah has made up her mind not to marry me." He frowned and looked at their joined hands. "But I'd like to keep that option open. I've just secured a new job. I'll be working the pipeline that's coming through the county this next year." He smiled. "They've hired me on as manager."

"Oh, William, that's wonderful news," Mrs. Douglas said, squeezing her husband's arm and smiling at him.

"Of course it will mean a lot of travel for me. I'll be going back and forth from here to the coast for the next few years." He frowned and looked towards Savannah. He couldn't really read what was on her face, but he had never really been able to tell what she was thinking. "I'd like to be a part of the child's life, of Savannah's life, if she'll have me."

Everyone waited and looked at Savannah.

"I can't make any promises," she said, coolly.

"Fair enough." He nodded, expecting it. "I'd like to at least be part of the baby's life. A child should know their father."

He waited and when Savannah nodded, he felt like he'd won the battle.

"Good, then here's what I propose." He turned to her parents. "I've purchased a new house." He smiled. "Sheriff Miller sold me his old place on Magnolia. I'd like Savannah to move in with me."

He heard Savannah gasp, and he glanced at her but didn't give her time to respond.

"We'd live together until I head out, then she and the baby can have the house to themselves until I return home, which will be in about six months." He hated to be away for that long, but he knew it would be necessary for Savannah and the baby's future. "After that, I'll be on an odd schedule. I'll be working offshore for two weeks straight, then home for another two."

"You'll be working on the oil rigs in the gulf?" Mr. Douglas asked.

He nodded. "After we finish laying the initial pipes." He turned to Savannah again. "Will you move in with me?"

She shook her head, no, just as her father said, "Yes."

"No, I won't." She turned to her father.

"Savannah." He stood and looked down at her. "I know it is your mother's and my fault that you've found yourself in your position."

Savannah laughed. "Really, father, you had nothing to do with it," she said, sarcastically.

"I mean," he continued, "that you find yourself in your twenties, no job, no real education, pregnant, and unwed." He crossed his arms over his chest. "We spoiled you. We had our reasons." Mrs. Douglas stood and put her hand on her husband's arm and nodded. "But it ends now. You're old enough to make your own choices, but that doesn't stop us from helping you make them."

"What are you saying?" Savannah tried to get off the sofa; Billy reached down and helped her stand. She tried to swipe his hands away, but when she almost fell back, she dug her fingers into his arms and relied on him to stand up.

"Are you kicking me out?" Her voice rose.

Her father looked down at her and nodded. "In a manner of speaking, yes. Your mother and I have discussed it for some time now. We think that it's time you started living your own life. And since you've made your choice"—he nodded towards Billy—"you need to strike out on your own and make something of it. Did you think your mother and I would just raise your baby for you?"

Savannah took a step back and almost fell backwards onto the sofa. Billy wrapped his arms around her to steady her. Her stomach bumped into him and, for a moment, he enjoyed the feeling of his child next to him. It was the most humbling experience he'd ever had and at that moment, he knew he'd made the right decision. Even if it meant that Savannah would hate him for the rest of his life.

Jill Sanders

Chapter Three

She watched Billy bring in the last of her bags and felt like throwing something. How could her parents do this to her? Why would they?

She leaned her head back and closed her eyes. She'd argued with her father and mother until she felt faint. They wouldn't budge on their decision. Her mother had gone with her upstairs to pack her things in her bags that very evening.

Now, just a few hours after she'd driven up to her house, she was sitting in Billy's new house, on his new sofa, and thinking of a million ways to kill the father of her child.

He set the bag down just inside the front door and walked over and sat next to her. "Do you know what it is?" He nodded towards her belly, looking like he wanted to reach out and touch it. She shook her head.

"I asked not to know." She put her hands over her large belly and hated the emotions she saw in his eyes.

"Why?" He reached his hand out and laid it over her large stomach.

She pushed up from the sofa and he put his hand on her waist to help her stand. She pushed it away when she finally stood. "My choice. Now, where is my room?" She turned to him and glared at him.

He chuckled. "Our room is just down there." He nodded towards the small hallway. It was so narrow, she doubted she would be able to walk down it with the extra weight she'd gained in the last few weeks. But since she didn't want to show any weakness, she bent down and picked up the lighter of the two bags and started walking towards the backroom. Billy ripped the bag from her hands halfway across the room.

"That's too heavy for you." He frowned. "You shouldn't be lifting it." He bent and picked up the other bag easily. She watched the muscles in his arms strain and wanted to reach out to play her fingers over them, but held herself still instead.

"I can take care of myself." She crossed her arms over her chest and watched his eyes focus on her large bosom. It had been the bane of her existence. She knew there were rumors going around that she'd had several enhancements, but the truth was, she was just very large. Even more so since the pregnancy. Actually, before finding out she was pregnant, she'd been looking into getting a reduction. Her back hurt her some days, so much so that she'd taken to seeing a chiropractor and a physical therapist twice a week. Her parents had even bought her an orthopedic mattress to help out. She doubted that Billy had something like that in what would no doubt be a very small bedroom, and she desperately wished to be back home.

"I've never doubted it," Billy said smiling. He carried the two bags past her and easily walked down the narrow hallway, leaving her in the small living room alone.

She frowned at the place. It was too small. What did he expect her to do in such a small place? She looked around.

She wouldn't admit it to anyone, but she'd always liked the small, green, classically styled house that the sheriff had always lived in. She'd just never imagined that it was this small on the inside.

Maybe she was just being mean. After all, every place looked small compared to her family home. She frowned. Even the large house that the West sisters had grown up in paled in comparison to her home.

But when she followed Billy down the hallway and walked into the small bedroom, she felt like fainting. She was going to live here. With him. For who knew how long.

Billy stood next to a queen-sized bed, her two bags at his feet, as he smiled over at her.

"Well." He smiled. "What do you think?"

"I think I'm going to kill you," she growled out. "Why did you do that?" She crossed her arms over her chest.

"What?" He looked at her with his big brown eyes.

"You know what. I was doing fine all by myself. Why did you have to go to my parents?" She leaned back against the wall, not wanting him to see that her back was hurting her, not to mention that her feet were so swollen they felt on the verge of bursting from her shoes.

"Come on, Savvy." He smiled over at her, charm seeping from every pore of his body.

He knew she hated it when he called her that. No one else had the guts to use it.

She felt like throwing something at him. She wrapped her fingers around a small clock that sat on the dresser next to her and tossed it at his head.

It hit the wall just above his head, and he laughed and ducked the next item she threw at

44

him.

Then he was rushing towards her, wrapping her in his arms. For just a moment, she enjoyed the feeling of being held. Then she pushed him away and hit him on the chest. Feeling her hand bounce off his rock hard muscles, she hated him even more.

"Leave me alone," she screamed and pushed him away.

"Oh, come on." He pulled back and placed a hand over her stomach, causing her to hold very still. "I just want to do what's right." He frowned at her then smiled when he felt her stomach kick him back.

"See, even the baby hates you." She tried to push his hands away from her stomach, but he easily pushed her hands aside and placed his other hand over her stomach. His dark eyes went wide as their child kicked even more.

"Amazing." He looked up at her. "Does it hurt you?" he asked, stepping closer to her.

Her mouth had gone dry. How had she never realized how handsome he was before? She blinked a few times and shook her head no.

"Have you thought about names?" He smiled again when the child inside her tried to punch its way out of her skin. She groaned a little when she felt pressure on her bladder. Again, she shook her head, but this time she was lying.

"I…" She blinked a few times. "I need to go to the restroom." She turned and started walking towards an open door, praying that it was a bathroom.

When she stepped inside a nice-sized master bathroom, she sighed and shut the door behind her. She hadn't realized she was crying until the tears rolled down her neck.

She could hear him banging around in the next room, and when she opened her eyes, she looked at her reflection in the large mirror and frowned.

She was huge and fat. Why would Billy be treating her like he was? She no longer felt attractive.

Her face was far too fat now. Even her hands and feet were so swollen that she hadn't been able to wear jewelry or pretty shoes for months. She frowned down at the pair of flats she'd been wearing for the last few weeks. They were the only shoes she had that she could slip on and that didn't require her to bend down to tie them.

Walking closer to the mirror, she ran her hands over her stomach and felt the kid kick again. Rushing to the toilet, she emptied the bladder that he or she had been pushing up against. When she walked over and washed her hands, she couldn't stop the tears from coming.

How had she let her life take such a drastic turn? She leaned her head against the cool mirror and thought back to that night almost eight months ago and wondered why she was always a sucker for a sexy man in tight jeans.

Billy finished unpacking Savannah's bags and cleaning up the glass from the three items she'd thrown at his head. He couldn't help but laugh at her weak attempt. He was just grateful that she'd been too exhausted to do any real damage.

He'd seen all her energy drain from her after she'd come back downstairs with her mother trailing behind her with the two large bags.

Her father had promised to deliver some more items by the end of the week, but he didn't know where he was going to put it all.

The small house had come furnished, so he hadn't had to purchase a lot of stuff, but so far, he liked everything that was in it and planned on keeping it. At this point, though, he was willing to let her redecorate as she wanted.

He knocked on the bathroom door when it grew too quiet in the next room. "Are you okay?" he asked.

"I…I'm going to take a bath. Would you bring my small bag to the door?" she called back.

He walked over and grabbed the small bag that contained all her makeup and bottles.

"I've got it," he called out. When she opened the door a small crack, he pushed it until she stood back and glared at him.

"Are you all right?" He set the bag down on the countertop and looked at her. He could tell she'd been crying and instantly felt bad.

He took a few steps towards her, and she shook her head and put her hands on his chest. "Don't," she said, looking down at her hands. "I just want to be left alone." Then she looked up at him and he saw the steel return to her eyes. "Just because I'm here, doesn't mean I want to be, or that we're going to be some sort of a couple."

He took a step back and nodded. He'd expected this from her. "I know."

She nodded. "Good. Then you won't have any problems sleeping on the couch." Her chin came up.

He smiled. "There's a guest room."

"Good." She nodded. "Then you'll forgive me for turning in. I'm quite tired." She walked over to the bedroom door and waited until he stepped out.

He stopped just shy of the door and put a hand on the door to stop her from closing it in his face. "Just because you've made up your mind to hate me, doesn't mean I'll give up trying." He reached over and brushed a finger down her cheek and watched her eyes go soft for a split second. "Goodnight, Savvy." He smiled and stepped through the door.

He chuckled when she slammed it in his face.

As he walked into the living room, he couldn't help but smile when he realized his plan was working.

He sat down on the sofa and crossed his arms over his chest. He'd been hurt when she'd shunned him. After all, he'd had a secret thing for Savannah for as long as he could remember. But the friend code had forced him to keep it hidden for years. Savannah and Travis had been an on-again, off-again thing for years. Even when Travis had been engaged to Alexis West, he'd kept his distance from Savannah.

Closing his eyes, he remembered the first night he'd really felt something for her. It was so long ago, yet the memory was still fresh. So was the hurt that had come when she'd gotten in her car with Travis that night instead of him.

She'd walked into the room looking like a woman, not a sixteen-year-old, like so many other girls around him had. She'd held her head up high and had demanded the attention of everyone in the room and his teenage heart had skipped. She still made it skip when she looked a certain way.

Her outer beauty was definitely something to behold, but it was her inner glow and strength that he'd always admired most. Her words had hurt so much that night when she'd turned him down that he'd turned back to his old ways. There was a little of his father in him after all.

He'd tried for so many years to deny the fact that he was like his father, but the more he embraced his rough edges, the better off he was. He'd been on a slow path to destruction before that night Travis had knocked some sense into him. It was funny; Travis had always been the instigator, but now he was the one who was most in control of his life.

Shaking his head, he chuckled. If anyone had said that would be the case in high school, they would have beaten them up. Propping his feet on the coffee table, he drifted off, remembering the good old times they used to have.

When he woke, it was to a finger in his chest.

"Are you okay?" Savannah said over him.

His eyes opened and blinked a few times. For a moment, he couldn't remember where he was.

"Sure," he said after using his hands to wipe his face from the sweat that had built up during the night.

"You were screaming." She frowned down at him.

"No, I wasn't." He frowned and sat up as she sat next to him. She was wearing a large t-shirt and sweatpants that were a few sizes too big for her.

"Yes you were." She crossed her arms over her chest.

He closed his eyes and nodded. Of course he had been screaming. "Sorry," he grunted out. "I didn't mean to wake you."

"You didn't," she said, causing his eyes to open and zero back on her. She shrugged her shoulders. "The kid plays havoc with my bladder. I'm up at least four times a night."

He looked down at her large stomach and nodded.

"Why aren't you sleeping in the guest room?"

"I guess I fell asleep out here." He dropped his feet to the ground and ran his sweaty hands over his jeans.

"Well," she said, looking at him and tilting her head.

"Here." He stood and helped her up from the sofa. Keeping his hands on her hips a little longer than necessary, he smiled when he saw her eyes soften.

"I'm sorry," she said, looking down at her hands on his shoulders. "I know I'm big." She frowned.

He chuckled. "I don't mind." He put his thumb under her chin and pulled until she was looking at him. "It shows me that you're taking good care of junior here." He put his hand over her stomach.

51

She nodded and took a step back. "Well, goodnight." She started walking out of the room.

"Savvy?" He smiled when she turned and her eyes heated. "Sweet dreams." She nodded and walked down the hallway towards her room.

Chapter Four

Over the next few weeks, she stayed out of Billy's way as much as possible. He started his new job and she only saw him for a few hours every evening. During the weekends, she made a point to either be out of the house or locked in her room fast asleep.

She watched in horror as the scale went higher and higher as she got closer to her due date. No matter what she tried, she couldn't stop herself from eating everything in sight. She even found herself sneaking into the kitchen in the middle of the night and grabbing what she could without waking Billy.

Her doctor appointments were now scheduled

for once a week. Billy tried to make the appointments, but with his new job, he ended up just asking her about them when he finally got home at night. He wanted to know every detail and sometimes had more questions for the doctor than she had.

Now everyone in town knew that Billy was the father and that they were living together in the small green house. Every time she stepped out of the house, it seemed that someone was waving at her or wanting to have a conversation with her.

She was too tired to fight the gossip or to really care about it. She started staying inside the house as much as she could and hated going out or seeing anyone.

Several of her friends had tried to put together a baby shower, but she had quickly and quietly shut them down, claiming she would have one after the baby was born and they knew the sex.

Her mother had stopped by one day and delivered several larger items and boxes, including a bassinet and a stroller. She didn't doubt that they were of highest quality and from the biggest named stores, but she was just so tired of it all at this point. She wanted the kid out of her so she could start her life over again.

She'd unpacked a few boxes of gifts from family members and friends that her mother had delivered. She hadn't really focused on what she was doing or the items she was putting away. Half of her closet was now baby clothes and the other half were clothes she no longer fit into. She found it all so comical that she didn't even care anymore.

Most days she just lay around on her uncomfortable bed and stared up at the ceiling, dreaming she was somewhere else. Someone else.

When she'd gone into the store one day to get milk, she'd overheard some high school students talking about her. She'd stopped at the end of the aisle and listened as they talked about how Billy probably had a temper like his old man and would end up beating her.

"That's probably why she doesn't come outside anymore," one of them had said. "It's a shame. When I get married, I'll never let my husband raise a hand to me."

Savannah felt like laughing. Billy? Hit her? She shook her head. There couldn't be anything farther from the truth. In fact, since she'd moved into the house, he'd done everything he could to make sure she was comfortable, short of delivering her king-sized mattress. He claimed the room was just too small for the larger bed and that she'd have to make due until he could afford to buy something newer.

But as she walked the block and a half back to the house, she couldn't help feel guilty for the gossip. She was being a recluse after all, which was fueling all the gossip about them. She supposed it wouldn't hurt to be seen more. Then she looked down at her belly and frowned. Did she really care about what high school kids said about her and Billy anyway?

The month of December was a blur and, before she knew it, they were going over to her parents' house to have Christmas dinner. She hadn't slept very well the night before, and getting dressed had taken her twice as long as usual. Her back and legs hurt more than ever and she desperately wished the kid would hurry up so she could get her body back.

When they drove up to her parents' place, she closed her eyes as Billy walked around the car to open her door. She wanted her bed badly, but knew her mother would be disappointed if she didn't spend the evening with them.

Getting out, she tried to ignore how nice it felt to have someone help her out of the car. Actually, Billy had been nothing but sweet and helpful since she'd moved into the green house. She rubbed her hand over her lower back and smiled a little when he was there to help her climb the few steps into her old house.

After the huge dinner, which she'd only nibbled on, they sat around the living room talking about Billy's job. She wasn't really paying attention to the conversation, since her lower back had started shooting pain all throughout her legs. Then she felt the gush of water rushing down her green leggings and gasped.

Her mother jumped up quickly and rushed to

her side, asking a million questions. Before she could answer any of them, pain shot through her entire body, this time there was no denying the labor pains.

Her eyes closed as she tried to control her breathing, then she felt her body being lifted in strong arms. The cool night air hit her face and she opened her eyes. She looked over at Billy as he carried her out towards his truck.

"Hang on." His dark eyes were on hers, and then his smile wavered as he saw the pain in her eyes. "I'll get you to the hospital quickly."

She nodded just as another pain hit her. She tried to roll her body up into a ball, but the pain was too much to move. She felt like everything was being ripped apart. Her back, her stomach, all of it was on fire.

She vaguely heard her parents tell Billy they'd meet him at the clinic, but she was too focused on the pain.

She felt his arms wrap around her as he buckled her seat belt, but then another kind of pain hit her. Pressure. She tried to push off the seat belt as a wave of urgency hit her.

"No," she cried out. "Too close," she said between gritted teeth. "Too soon," she tried to tell him, grabbing his hands.

"What?" he said, looking off towards her parents' car as they sped out of the driveway.

"The baby's coming now." She pushed her Christmas leggings down her legs. "Billy, now!" she cried out.

"It can't be happening this quick." His face paled as he watched her in horror.

"Now!" she screamed. She flung off the seat belt, grabbed his hand, and put her legs up on his dash. She took a deep breath and closed her eyes as another wave of pain hit her.

"Oh…my…God," she heard him say, putting long spaces in between each word. Then she felt his hands on her thighs as he helped her hold her legs up. "Here it comes." She heard his voice waver.

When she opened her eyes, she noticed that he'd removed his new Christmas jacket and was holding it under her, ready to take the baby.

She leaned her head back and groaned with another sharp pain. "Billy?" She reached out and took his hand. "I'm scared." She looked into his deep eyes and saw his fear there as well. He nodded and tried to smile.

Just then she heard a car drive up, and she closed her eyes when she heard her parents rush back towards them.

"What the…" Her father stopped a few feet away.

"Now," Billy said. "It's happening now. Help." He looked towards her mother who just stood there, smiling.

"You can do this," her mother said eagerly. She shocked them by climbing in next to Savannah in the truck instead of taking over for Billy. Her mother smiled down at her. "Both of you can do this." She nodded to Billy who looked back down at the little head that was coming out as Savannah pushed one more time.

"I've got her," Billy said, laughing. "It's a girl." He laughed again as he wrapped the little white and red blotchy baby in his new two hundred dollar wool coat. "She's beautiful." He smiled up at her.

"Here." Her father stepped forward and handed him a bobby pin and a knife. "To cut the cord." He shrugged his shoulders. "It's all I could find quickly." He smiled and looked down at the small bundle in Billy's arms.

"Hold her." He reached up and handed Savannah the bundle. At first Savannah wanted to push the child away, but before she could say anything, he was setting the bundle on her lap as he used the bobby pin and knife to cut the cord.

Savannah looked down at the wet mess that was her child and then the little girl opened her dark eyes and she felt something shift inside her. She felt something she hadn't known was possible. Pure love. Love at first sight.

Billy paced in the waiting room and walked quickly back and forth. He'd gone to the restroom and had cleaned up as much as he could. His dress shirt and pants were completely ruined, but he didn't mind. He ran his hands through his hair one more time.

Savannah's parents had given up on trying to get him to calm down. He wouldn't feel calm until he could see his girls again.

Hearing the clinic doors open, he smiled as Travis and Holly walk in.

"Well?" his friend asked, shaking his hand and patting him on his shoulder.

"It's a girl." He smiled and laughed when his friend pulled him close and hugged him right there in front of everyone in the waiting room.

"Congratulations." Travis laughed. "Heard you had her in the car." He shook his head and laughed.

"Yeah, Maggie couldn't wait."

"Maggie?" Holly asked.

"Yeah, Maggie Elizabeth Jackson." He smiled.

"Good name." Holly smiled. "Did you pick it out or Savannah?"

He chuckled. "I haven't run it by her yet." He turned and looked at the swinging doors that led down the hallway towards the private rooms. "If they let me back there soon, I will."

Just then Melissa West walked in from the back, wearing her scrubs. "Billy?" She walked towards him just as Mr. and Mrs. Douglas stood up. "You can go back now. Room three." She smiled and then looked over towards Savannah's parents. "The room is too small for everyone at once."

"That's okay," Savannah's mother said. "We'll wait."

Billy turned to Travis. "Will you wait around? Maybe they'll let me bring her out and show her off." Travis nodded.

When Billy walked into room three, he blinked a few times to let his eyes adjust to the darker room. He could see Savannah sitting up in the bed, holding a small bundle.

"Hey," he said, walking towards her. She looked up and smiled.

"She's just having her first meal." She nodded down to the dark head that was at her breast.

He walked over and sat on the bed next to her and looked in amazement at his daughter.

"Are you okay?" he asked, looking at Savannah.

"Sure." She didn't look up from the baby. "The doctor checked us out and we're clean and clear to go home tomorrow."

"That's good." He frowned a little. "So, I was thinking about names."

She looked up at him. "I know. Margaret." She nodded. "Maggie. I know," she repeated and then smiled. "I like it."

He chuckled. "I guess I was talking a little too loud out there." He nodded towards the waiting room.

She chuckled and shook her head. "No, I saw the scratch paper where you'd written a list of names the other day in the kitchen." She looked back down at the baby. "Maggie is perfect."

"Yes." He smiled. "Yes, she is."

Chapter Five

Over the next few weeks, Savannah felt like packing a small bag, leaving alone, and never looking back. Anyone who said that being a new mother was easy was lying. Not only did her body hurt, but now she was expected to live on only a few hours of sleep each night.

And she'd had to change more diapers than she cared to mention. It wasn't as if she hadn't changed a baby's diapers before, just never this many. It seemed like every time she turned around, Maggie was wet or dirty again. Eating, sleeping, crying, and messing her diapers seemed to be all her baby did.

Billy, for his part, was staying clear of her ever since she had chewed him out about buying the wrong sized diapers. When he did help her out with Maggie, he was always very gentle with the baby and never stopped smiling. She found it quite annoying since she was moody and tired all of the time.

Maybe it was because her breasts, which had almost doubled in size during pregnancy, were now even bigger due to the milk. She'd almost given up on breast-feeding altogether, but little Maggie was a champ at it and would usually suck her dry and still want more.

When she wasn't dealing with Maggie, she was sleeping. She took more naps during the day than she could ever remember taking as a child. Her emotions were swinging all over the place and at times, she found herself crying for no reason at all. But every time she thought about all the difficulty she was going through, all she had to do was hold the little girl and her heart would melt a little.

Since Billy had taken off a few weeks of work, he had gotten some things done around the house that needed to be handled. He'd replaced the dishwasher with a new one, had fixed a window that had leaked the last rain they'd had, and had even moved in a new mattress for Savannah and Maggie.

She had to admit that she was grateful when he started going back in to work. He was always so overly happy about everything and it was getting on her nerves.

She just couldn't bring herself to leave the little

girl in the crib that sat across the small room from her bed. Instead, at night, she would lay the little girl next to her and fall asleep holding her. She knew everyone had told her it wasn't a good habit, but she just couldn't fall asleep without feeling Maggie's little heart beat next to hers.

Before she knew it, she had fallen into a pattern and had completely forgotten the life she used to live. Her friends stopped calling her and asking if she wanted to go out. The only people she saw outside of her small home were her family.

When she'd watched Billy drive away to leave town for work, she'd felt a little sadness knowing he'd be gone for the next several months.

One day, a few weeks after he'd left, she'd gone into the Grocery Stop and had bumped into several high school girls. She couldn't remember their names, but knew one of them was the captain of the cheer squad this year. She'd seen them practicing the last time she'd gone out to the school to help with a fundraiser. She thought back and realized it had been almost a year since she'd done anything like that. She used to be on top of every event that went on in town and had been Fairplay's biggest event supporter until just a few months before Maggie was born.

Now she moved aside and apologized to the pair, making sure to tuck Maggie closer to her chest in the cotton wrap that hung around her front. She continued to push her almost full cart and hunt the aisles for what she needed. When she reached the end of the aisle, she heard the girls giggling and turned back just in time to hear the tall brunette say loud enough for her to hear,

"That's her. I hear the father of the baby took off right after it was born. I guess he couldn't stand having both of them under one roof."

The blonde girl looked over at Savannah and smiled as her eyes ran up and down her, and then she giggled. "Can you blame him. I mean, look at her."

The brunette nodded and giggled along as they walked out of the store without buying anything.

Savannah tried to shake it off and moved to continue her shopping. She was used to being gossiped about, especially in her own hometown. Besides, she told herself, it didn't matter what a couple of dumb high school girls thought of her anyway.

But when she moved to the freezer aisle and grabbed a half gallon of her new Blue Bunny favorite, Cookies and Cream, she caught a glance of her reflection in the glass and gasped.

Staring back at herself, she felt the tears build up behind her eyes. It had been almost two months since Maggie had been born and she hadn't lost a single pound of the weight she'd gained. Well, okay, she'd probably lost a pound, but to be honest, she hadn't had the nerve to get on the old scale that sat in her bathroom.

Her hair was a mess and hadn't been colored or cut for over six months, so naturally, her silky blonde locks were dull and raggedy. Not to mention that she'd left the house without even drying her hair, so the mass of it was tied up in a large bun on the very top of her head.

She looked more closely at her reflection and frowned. She wasn't wearing any makeup. She had never left the house without makeup before. Never.

She left her full cart in the freezer aisle, and walked towards the front of the grocery store.

But when she went to walk around the checkout stands, the clerk, Carmen, a girl Savannah had gone to school with, stopped her.

"Is everything okay?" She stepped in front of her. Carmen was a little taller than Savannah. Her long dark hair was braided and hung over her shoulder. Her rich brown eyes were full of concern.

Savannah felt her eyes start to water and wanted the cool air outside. She didn't cry often, but when she did, she did it in privacy.

She nodded her head and tried to walk around Carmen, who just put a hand on her shoulders. "Savannah, is there anything I can help with?"

Just hearing those words caused the damn walls to crack and before she knew it, she was blabbering and wailing to this stranger standing in the front of the Grocery Stop for all to hear. Maggie was still strapped to the stroller in front of her.

Carmen took her shoulders and walked her to a small room in the front of the store. She handed her a box of tissues.

"I know how bad hormones can be. I've got a boy and a girl myself." Carmen smiled and nodded to a framed picture of two small kids. "Did those girls say something to set this all off?"

Savannah shook her head. "What do I care about what some dumb high school kids think." Savannah sniffled again.

Carmen chuckled. "That sounds like the old Savannah I know."

She looked up at her and frowned. "You know me?"

Carmen laughed. "My whole life. Now, I'll give you some advice that someone gave me once a long time ago. Listen to what others say about you..."—she held up her hand and stopped Savannah from speaking—"Listen, but don't take it to heart. If what they say is true, and you agree with them and have it in your power to change, then change."

Savannah frowned at her and hiccuped. "That's really terrible advice."

Carmen smiled and nodded. "It works great when the thing you're changing is the pair of jeans your parents bought you, but not so well in all other matters."

"I didn't give you that advice did I?"

Carmen laughed even more and nodded. "Yes. You thought I should wear skinny jeans instead of boot cut." She shrugged her shoulders and patted her capri pants. "So, I changed to something I felt comfortable with."

Savannah laughed and instantly felt better.

"Thank you." She blew her nose again.

"For?" Carmen frowned a little.

Savannah shrugged her shoulders. "I haven't talked to anyone for a while. Like this." She sighed.

Carmen laughed. "Well, I'm here five days a week." Then she sighed and Savannah watched as sadness crept into her eyes. "Maybe starting six or seven days soon."

When she got home, she gently put Maggie down in her crib and walked into her bathroom and stood in front of the mirror. She was still wearing her maternity clothes, so they weren't stylish at all. Not to mention they were huge. She sighed. *She* was still huge.

Removing her clothes, she stood before the mirror again. Her body was a mess. There were stretch marks down the inner sides of her thighs. She still had a pooch on her stomach and when her eyes moved up to her breasts, she sighed. Would they ever go back down?

The final straw in all this mess was the fact that her long beautiful blonde hair was falling out. Not just a few strands here and there, but handfuls of it came out each time she showered.

She felt like screaming. But instead, she stood in her bathroom and looked at herself for a long time.

"Get it together, Savannah," she said and watched her reflection. "You can do this." She lifted her arms and felt her stomach roll as she watched in horror as the skin under them flapped.

In that moment, she decided it was time she woke up. She used to love working out. After all, she'd wanted to make sure everyone looked at her and liked what they saw.

She knew all it would take is her doing it. She had asked about exercise during her last doctor appointment, and had been told she could get back to her normal routine. So why hadn't she started?

She started to stretch. Her muscles were sore at first, but it felt really good to use them again.

Over the next few days, she cleaned the small kitchen of junk food. When she went to the store this time, she focused on buying only fresh vegetables. She had at one point been a vegetarian, and now when she walked up to the checkout, she realized she hadn't bought any meat and didn't care. The last time she'd stopped eating meat, she'd lost a few pounds in the first week. It couldn't hurt.

She even picked up a workout DVD that she'd seen at the checkout stand and had started working out to it in the living room while Maggie lay in the small crib next to her.

She enjoyed cooking with the fresh ingredients and had gotten on her laptop to find new recipes she would enjoy.

She drove Maggie into Tyler and purchased a couple workout outfits and a new pair of running shoes. She had to try on a few to get the right size and was shocked when she saw the double-digit sizes she now wore; she'd always been a size three before. To take her mind off of herself, she had hunted the baby section and had bought Maggie a few things, which had instantly cheered her up.

A few weeks later, once she felt her energy growing, she took out the stroller her parents had purchased for her and started taking long walks with Maggie. She'd bundled the little girl up tight as she walked in the cool weather. Maggie seemed to enjoy it.

One day, she was late in leaving for her walk and Maggie started fussing. When she sat her in the stroller, finally, she settled down and began to smile and kick her feet excitedly.

"There's my girl." She smiled. "You like to

work out with mommy?" She laughed as she took off at a slight jog. She was thinking of driving into town and purchasing one of the strollers she could run behind. This one, she could only jog slowly and walk with.

She couldn't really tell if her body was changing, only that she felt more levelheaded and more energetic when she worked out.

Every time she went to the grocery store, she would visit with Carmen, who worked there almost every day. Funny, she really didn't remember much about Carmen in high school, only that she'd been short, a little mousy, and unpopular enough not to warrant an invite to most of Savannah's parties. But, now, each time she saw her, they ended up talking more and more. Carmen was a mother of two, a boy and a girl, both in elementary school. She was going through a nasty divorce and her husband was trying to get out of paying her anything, even though he'd talked her into giving up a full scholarship to Stephen F. Austin University to raise the kids. Now she was living with her parents and working at the Grocery Stop, just to make ends meet.

Hearing Carmen's story really helped her see that it wasn't just her that had been dealt a blow. Other people actually had it worse. Savannah found herself stopping in the Grocery Stop more often just to chat with Carmen.

It had been almost two months since Billy had

left town for work. He called her almost every evening and she filled him in on everything about Maggie. She'd snapped pictures of them on her phone and sent them to his cell when he requested. He would send funny pictures of himself back and she'd show them to Maggie while he talked to the little girl on speakerphone.

She felt herself growing fonder of him as time went by. They often spent time talking to one another, and she was really enjoying hearing his voice every evening. She missed his calls when he wasn't able to make them, and had even played a few voice messages for Maggie when the little girl would fuss. They always seemed to calm the baby down and helped her mind settle as well.

She hadn't told him anything about her workouts, feeling like it would somehow overstep the personal line she'd drawn months ago.

He would talk to her about his work and the men he was in charge of. She found most of it boring, but he would often entertain her with a funny story of the men goofing off.

She wondered if he went out with the other men on the weekends. She knew that he'd run around with several other women in town after they'd discovered she was pregnant. Every time Billy and Corey had gone out, news had spread fast in the small town, mostly because they were usually in trouble. But somehow she doubted that he had continued his ways now that he was in charge of the work crew. And now that he was a father.

She fell into a pattern. For the most part, she stayed to herself in the tiny house, just her and Maggie. Her parents would stop by and give almost all of their attention to the little baby. She didn't mind, since it allowed her to relax a little. Her mother kept bringing Maggie gifts and the little girl's room was quickly filling up with too much stuff. She thought about arranging everything and maybe even decorating it, but just couldn't bring herself to believe that they would be living in the small place for very long.

She really started enjoying her daily walks. Even though the weather had forced her to take them early or late in the day because of the pounding heat, she struck out each time with a smile on her face and enjoyed the way moving cleared her head.

She'd enjoyed taking the back roads just outside of town more than walking down the busy streets of row houses and people.

The old highway bridge had always been one of her favorite places to go. The old highway wasn't used anymore and the old bridge sat high over a slow moving stream. There was plenty of fish and turtles in the water and she just loved watching them move about in the clear water.

On several occasions during the evenings, she'd come across the same young girl sitting on the bridge. At first, Savannah only nodded as she walked by, but one evening, she noticed that the girl was crying. Her face was bright red and her eyes were soaked. When she noticed Savannah, she frantically wiped her nose and eyes on the inside sleeve of her shirt.

"Are you okay, sweetie?" Savannah stopped and took a good look at the girl for the first time.

She was very thin and pale. She had braces and her auburn hair was matted and pulled back in a loose ponytail. Her clothes were baggy and not stylish at all.

When the young girl looked up at her and nodded, Savannah's first thought was that she would have instantly made fun of the girl had she been in school with her. Then she took a closer look and noticed that her big blue eyes were sad. Very sad. No matter what her initial thoughts were, Savannah remembered seeing the same look in her own eyes just a few short months ago.

Pulling Maggie's stroller around, she parked it near where the young girl was sitting along the old wood planks. Her feet were dangling off the edge of the bridge. Savannah squatted down and sat next to her.

"It's a pretty spot you have here." She looked off to the slow flowing water below them. A handful of turtles jumped into the water quickly.

When the girl remained silent, she looked over at her. "I'm Savannah Douglas."

She watched the girl nod. "Everyone knows who you are." Her voice was just a whisper.

Savannah laughed. "Don't believe half of the stuff you hear about me." She leaned closer to the young girl and realized she was a little older than she'd first gauged. "For example, these…"—she pointed to her chest and smiled—"are real."

The girls jaw dropped and when Savannah smiled at her again, the girl laughed a little.

"Seriously?"

"Yup." Savannah couldn't stop herself from laughing, but then she frowned a little. "But I did recently get a nose job." She reached up and played with the tip of her nose, remembering the incident. "But that was only because someone punched me in the face." She laughed when she realized that she'd deserved it.

"What about you?" She looked at the girl who sniffled and looked off towards the water.

"Kids at school make fun of me. Of the way I dress, of how I look. They call me…" She paused and closed her eyes. "Greasy Tracy."

"Is that your name?" She quickly added, "Tracy?"

The girl nodded without opening her eyes. "You know, kids can be pretty stupid." She sighed. "I should know. I used to be one of them. And until recently, I never really thought about how I'd hurt someone else." She shook her head. "I wouldn't listen too closely to what anyone has to say about you."

"Yeah, well…" Tracy stood up and dusted off her jeans. "What would you know; you've never been on my end of things." The girl started walking away and Savannah's heart sunk a little.

"Tracy." The girl stopped. "I'm currently on your side of things. I have no friends." She shrugged her shoulders. "The whole town is gossiping about me, saying mean and hurtful things to the point where I spend most of my days alone in a small house with the only person who loves me." She nodded to her sleeping daughter in her stroller. "And that's probably only because she doesn't know any better yet." She gave a half smile to the young girl. "But look at me." She motioned to herself. "I still get up every day, take a walk, and enjoy life. I listen to what people say about me and if what they say is true and I don't like those things about myself, I change them. If what they are saying isn't true"—she smiled and looked down at her large breasts—"then I just ignore them and hold my head up high and let them think what they want."

Tracy looked at her for the longest time. "I better get back home." She looked down at her feet and kicked a pebble into the water below.

Savannah felt her heart sink and realized she hadn't gotten through to the girl.

"Will you be here tomorrow?" The girl glanced

up through a thick strand of dark hair.

Savannah's smile was quick as she nodded. "I usually take my walks about this time. I can be here, if you want."

Tracy took a few steps in the opposite direction. "Yeah, I guess that would be cool."

She turned and started walking away without another word.

Over the next few weeks, Savannah and Tracy hung out on the bridge a handful of times. Each time Savannah tried to crack her shell and get through to her. She didn't know if what she was saying was helping or hurting, but she knew she was slowly making a friend and hoped that somehow she could reverse some of the damage she'd done in her youth by talking to the girl.

One day, during her walk, she was pushing Maggie's stroller past the bookstore when Holly rushed out of the front door and raced towards her.

"Savannah," she called to her as she jogged across the street towards her. When she reached her, the slender redhead was almost breathless. "Wow, you walk fast." She smiled at her.

Savannah nodded a little. She'd known Holly her entire life, but had never really paid too much attention to the bookstore owner. The fact that she was the one who had broken her nose only last year still didn't sit well with her. She tensed a little as the woman stopped right beside her. "I'm trying to burn off some of the baby fat."

"Well, you certainly have." Holly smiled and Savannah had to admit, the woman had turned beautiful, despite how she had looked as a child. "You look wonderful," Holly said, leaning down and looking at Maggie. "I can't believe how fast she's grown." She brushed a hand over Maggie's hair. "Her hair has lightened up. She looks so much like you." Holly smiled up at her. "But, I think she has her daddy's dark eyes." She cooed and let Maggie take her finger in her chubby hand.

"Really?" Savannah walked around to the front of the stroller and looked down at her daughter. She hadn't noticed it, but it was true. Maggie's hair had lightened quite a lot since her birth. Now, she could see some of herself in the chubby cheeks and smiled.

"Yes, I noticed she had Billy's eyes right away." Holly said, smiling down at Maggie, and Savannah felt a jolt of pride rush over her. "Would you like to come in?" Holly nodded towards her shop.

Holly's business was the local bookstore, coffeehouse, and wine bar all rolled into one. Savannah had been inside a few times since Holly and Travis had opened back up after a full remodel of the building, but she had never been there when they were in the shop. Instead, she'd always made sure that one of the employees, April or Karlene, were working instead.

Now as she looked over at the tall building,

which sat only a few blocks from her house, she could see the place was full of people. She took a step back. "Well…" She tried to think of an excuse. Any excuse.

"Oh, please. I'm really sorry about breaking your nose," she blurted out.

Savannah looked at her and realized the woman was as sincere as she could get.

Savannah nodded but remembered the pain and embarrassment. She knew now that she'd probably deserved it.

Holly sighed and looked off towards the bookstore. "Maggie would love seeing the other children. Besides, we're just about to start reading time." Holly smiled.

"Reading time?"

"Sure, we take time each week to read to the younger kids. You wouldn't think of it to look at our town, but there are loads of smaller children here." She smiled. "We have reading days, craft days, and even mommy break days." She smiled.

"Mommy break days?" She walked back behind the stroller and thought about retreating.

"Sure, mommies need a break. Every Thursday morning, from nine to noon, we watch the kids so mommies can have a few hours to themselves." She smiled and started walking back towards the building. "You'll enjoy it. Besides, Maggie needs to be introduced to some of the other kids in town."

Savannah frowned. Holly had a point. So far, Maggie hadn't been around any other kids. Was she stiffing her daughter? She thought of Tracy and how she'd tried to encourage the girl. Maybe she should be taking some of her own advice and putting herself out there more.

Nodding, she followed Holly towards the building. She was going to give her daughter a social life, even if it meant she had to play nice with the other parents in the process. Her daughter was worth the awkwardness of having to deal with people gossiping about her and looking at her funny the way they always did.

When they walked into the building, every mother stopped talking and looked towards them. She straightened her shoulders and tried to put on her social smile.

"Everyone, this is Maggie," Holly said as she gently pulled the baby from the stroller.

Everyone said, "Oh," in unison, and then several women rushed towards them, and Maggie was whisked into the arms of the other mothers.

"I'm glad you came." Savannah turned and saw Lauren West standing next to her, a chubby boy of almost two on her hip. She knew it was her sister Alexis' son, Gavin. She and Alex had never really gotten along, but at one point, way back in grade school, Lauren and Savannah had been best

81

friends.

She set the boy down and he waddled off towards a pile of toys that sat in the middle of a group of kids. "What do you say to a cup of tea and some crumb cake?" She tugged on Savannah's hand until she followed her to the bar area. "You've met April?"

Savannah nodded at the tall blonde woman who had pink streaks in her hair. "I've watched you run by the window almost every day." April smiled. "But I've never thought to run after you." She smiled. "It looked like Holly was going to chase you down and tackle you to get you to stop." She laughed and set a cup of warm tea in front of her.

Savannah went to push the tea away. "I'm nursing."

"It's okay, honey, it's caffeine free." April winked. "Drank truckloads of this stuff while I was nursing my kids."

Savannah nodded and took the cup. She frowned when Lauren sat a large slice of cranberry crumb cake in front of her.

"Oh, I don't think—" she started.

"Hush now. You may not see it, but you're skinnier now than ever before." Lauren smiled. "It's always hard to bounce back after a baby, but somehow you've managed to do it in only a few months, and I'll bet without going to the gym once." She shook her head and frowned a little.

"Kind of makes me sick." Then she laughed.

Savannah looked down at herself. She was very proud of the progress she'd made. She was back into the clothes she'd worn prior to getting pregnant and some of them were a little loose on her.

"Besides, you deserve a break." She leaned on the bar. "Look at her." She smiled. "She's enjoying herself."

Savannah took a little nibble of cake and turned around to see her daughter smiling as she was held by Haley, Lauren's youngest sister. There were twin boys standing next to her making funny faces at Maggie, who was giggling like Savannah had never heard before.

The sound brought a tear to her eyes.

"Oh, honey." Lauren took her arm. "Is everything okay?"

Savannah looked over at her and nodded. "I guess I'm just hormonal." She used the napkin Lauren had given her to dry her eyes.

Lauren smiled. "Comes with the job." She chuckled. "Now, let's go sit down before the story begins."

Savannah nodded and took the cake and her cup of tea and followed Lauren to a small table near the kids.

Jill Sanders

Chapter Six

$\mathcal{A}$s Billy listened to Savannah talk about Tracy and story time at Holly's, he wished more than anything that he was back at home. He never should have taken this job. The hours were long and the work was back breaking. Even though he was a supervisor, he still walked into his hotel room each night with more aches and pains than he cared for.

Most of the men were hard workers, but a handful of them were just plain stupid. Actually, a few of them reminded him of himself just a few short months ago.

He missed his girls. Even though they would Skype every night, he missed holding his daughter, missed smelling her hair after bath time. She was growing so fast. In every picture Savannah sent, he could see the subtle changes in her face.

He'd cried after hanging up with them one night

after Maggie had laughed and cooed for him. He desperately wished he'd been there in person to see it. Her little eyes lit up, and she was kicking her hands and feet now, making it look like she wanted him to hold her. Only three more months to go until he could go home and get on a more normal schedule.

A few days later, he received a call that sent shivers down his bones. He picked up the phone after being called to the main office.

"This is William Jackson."

"Well, well. You're a hard man to track down, William Jackson, Jr." Just hearing the voice gave him chills.

"What do you want?" he asked, reaching over and shutting the office door so no one else would hear the conversation.

"Heard you made it to the big time. Hitching up with the Douglas girl." His father chuckled and a million memories flooded his mind. None of them were pleasant.

"I'll repeat my question. What do you want?"

"Money," his father said, simply.

"You don't need money in the slammer." He almost hung up on him.

"I'm not in the slammer anymore." His father chuckled. "Actually, I was thinking of heading back into Fairplay. Maybe see that cute grandchild of mine."

"If you step foot in Fairplay…I'll…"

"What?" his father broke in. "I've served my time. I'm out on good behavior." He heard his father take a drink of something and knew without a doubt it was a shot of Jim Beam.

"How much?" he asked and closed his eyes. "How much do you want to stay away?"

"Ten thousand," his father said quickly. "That should keep me busy for a while." He chuckled again and Billy felt his skin crawl.

"Fine, tell me where." He wrote down the information quickly as his father gave it to him. "I'll wire it tomorrow." He hung up before his father could make any more demands.

Sitting down behind his desk, he rubbed his forehead and felt a headache building behind his eyes.

Two months couldn't go by quickly enough.

Savannah looked at herself in the mirror one last time. She couldn't explain why she was nervous, but she was. She must have changed outfits a half dozen times. She'd changed Maggie just as many times, but for different reasons. Maggie had wet the first one, and had thrown up a little on the second dress she'd picked.

Now, she leaned forward and applied just a little clear lip gloss to her lips and smiled. "There. Perfect."

She'd changed so much in the last few months. Living alone with just Maggie as company had made her look inward. She hadn't liked the person she'd become and just like dropping a few pounds, she'd decided to drop a few tendencies she had. And she owed it all to Maggie.

She looked down at the little girl, who smiled and tried to grab the fuzzy frogs that hung over her head in her carrier. "Shall we go get your daddy?"

Maggie squealed at the word "daddy," like she always did. Savannah laughed and picked up the carrier. Maggie was getting so heavy, it took both of her arms to hold her and the carrier now. She set the carrier in the stroller, grabbed her purse, and locked up the house.

"Morning, Savannah," she heard before she reached the end of her walk. "How's Maggie today?" Mrs. Cole rushed over from her yard as fast as her eighty-year-old legs could carry her and started cooing at Maggie. "She sure is growing so fast. I do believe she's grown another inch since I saw her yesterday."

Savannah laughed. "Mrs. Cole, I think it's time you had your eyesight checked." They laughed.

"Going to get Billy from the bus station today?"

Savannah nodded.

"Well, won't it be wonderful to have your daddy back in town," Mrs. Cole said to Maggie. "Well, you two better get going. I thought I saw the bus pass by a few minutes ago."

Savannah looked down the street with worry. "Thanks. See you later." She pushed the stroller quickly down the sidewalk and hoped that she hadn't left Billy waiting too long.

Halfway down the next block, she spotted him walking towards them. He looked a little thinner and a little taller, if that was possible.

"Billy," she called out, and he lifted his eyes from the ground to them. Then he was smiling and running towards them.

He jogged a little and met him in the middle.

"Hey." He smiled at her and dropped his bags.

All of a sudden, a bout of awkwardness rushed over her. She didn't know if she should hug him or not. He made the decision for her and pulled her into his arms and kissed her right there on the street. She felt her heart jump and her pulse skip. Then he released her and knelt down to pull Maggie from her stroller.

She used that time to get her breathing back under control. She had never reacted to him like this before. For that matter, she'd never reacted to anyone like that before.

"I can't believe how big she is." He tried to hold Maggie like he'd done when she was a baby, but Maggie was having none of it and kept trying to sit up in his arms.

Savannah chuckled. "She likes to be held like this." She walked over and helped him turn her around. "There, now she can see you."

Maggie's little hands came up and rested on his chin as he smiled down at her. He laughed when she reached up and put his chin in her mouth.

"Sorry," Savannah laughed. "The doctor says she's teething."

"What?" He chuckled and looked up at her. "So soon?"

"She is just over six months old." She smiled and waved at someone who honked as they drove by.

His eyes were on her and she saw him smiling at her.

"What?" she asked, feeling self-conscious.

"Look at you." His eyes ran over her and he frowned a little.

"What?" She frowned back and looked down at herself. "Did Maggie mess up this shirt as well?"

He shook his head and held Maggie tighter. "No, you look good." His voice softened and lowered, causing her face to flush as she smiled.

"We have a surprise for you." She smiled. "But we'll have to drop off your bags first." She nodded to the discarded duffel bags that lay on the sidewalk.

He nodded and bent down to pick up the bigger of the bags. "Toss that one on her stroller will you? I want to carry my girl for a while." He smiled and kissed Maggie's cheek.

Savannah picked up his bag and set it on the stroller and then walked beside him as he started back down the street.

"How was the trip back?" she asked, not sure what to talk to him about. Why was she feeling nervous? After all, it was just Billy. She'd known him her whole life. They'd slept together, made a baby together, and lived together. Why was she feeling nervous around him, like she didn't know him?

"It was okay. The bus had a flat tire just outside of Dallas." He shook his head and placed another kiss on Maggie's cheek, causing their daughter to squeal with glee.

"I hope you don't mind, but the sheriff stopped by one day and suggested I have the house painted, so I hired Corey to put a fresh coat on the place." She nodded to the house.

Corey, Billy's friend, had done a fantastic job, and he'd put a fresh coat of paint on the inside, as well.

"The place looks good. Corey texted me and filled me in." He smiled. "Who would have known he'd have the talent and patience to do that." He laughed.

She used her key and opened the front door. "He also did some work inside." She stepped in and set the stroller in its corner. "I hope you don't mind, but I moved a few things around." She nodded to the room.

He smiled. "Savvy, I told you, you can do whatever you want with the place." He set his bag down.

"Good, because I was reading this book about parenting, and well, Maggie needed her own room," she blurted out.

He turned to her, his dark eyebrows going up slowly. "Oh?" His smile spread a little.

She ignored his smile and walked past him. "Yes, well, I think you'll like it. Maggie loves it," she said nervously as she opened their daughter's room.

He stepped in with Maggie on his hip and smiled. "Frogs?" He laughed.

"Yes, well, it seems your daughter has a thing for the Princess and the Frog." She frowned a little.

"She does, does she?" He laughed.

She'd hated doing it, but painting her daughter's

room a light shade of green seemed to make Maggie happy. Every time she would hold up the pink swatch of paint in front of her daughter's face, she would reach for the green instead. When Savannah would hold up a picture of Cinderella, Savannah's favorite character, Maggie would cry and reach for the Princess and the Frog one instead.

There were two large wall stickers of frogs on the wall next to her crib and a frog mobile that hung over her daughter and played sweet chimes as she slept.

"I like it." He smiled. "If it makes my girls happy." He walked over and sat Maggie down on the floor and then sat next to her and handed her a stuffed frog. "I can't believe how big she is." He looked up at Savannah and smiled. "And how little you are." His eyes raked over her and she felt a wave of heat flood her entire body. "You look good." He stood up and started walking towards her. "Real good."

His hands grabbed her hips and pulled her closer to him. It had been so long since someone had touched her. Too long. She couldn't stop herself from melting into his arms.

He smiled down at her and she realized he did look taller. Her neck craned as she looked up at him. Then he dipped his head and his lips touched hers lightly.

The kiss was different than the one he'd given

to her on the street. It was different than any kiss he'd given her before.

They were adults. Her mind zeroed in on the thought. Everything else they'd done prior to this, they'd done as children. For the first time in her life, she felt like a real woman. Her arms wrapped around his neck and she pulled him closer, feeling her body heat next to his.

Then her cell phone rang and she jerked back. "Oh," she said, looking down at the screen. "I almost forgot." She pushed her hair away from her eyes. "We're going to be late for your surprise." She smiled and walked over to pick up Maggie.

He groaned. "Can't you just give me my surprise here?" he asked, reaching for her. She laughed and pulled away.

Billy tried to keep his mind on anything other than how sexy Savannah looked walking next to him. Even as he held his daughter in his arms, his eyes kept rushing back to her body. She was wearing tight black leggings with a long flowing gray shirt. She had on sexy gray ankle boots, which made her legs look even longer than he remembered. He felt a bead of sweat drip down between his shoulder blades. He doubted it had anything to do with the almost ninety-degree weather they were having.

He kept wondering what she was wearing underneath, but then his mind would snap to the fact that they were walking down the street in the middle of town.

"Here we are." She smiled and nodded towards the coffee shop. Holly's sat right on the corner across from Mama's diner, the only place in town to get a good meal. He hadn't been in Holly's since they'd remodeled a few months back, but he'd heard that the place was a huge success. He's also heard that Travis and Holly were now engaged.

"What are we doing here?" He reached out and took her hand in his to stop her.

She looked up at him and smiled. "You'll see."

As he looked down at her face, he realized how much she'd changed. She'd lost all the weight she'd gained when she was pregnant. Actually, it looked like she'd gone even farther down in size and he frowned a little at seeing just how skinny she really was.

She'd cut her hair a little shorter than the last time he'd seen her, and she'd colored it a little darker. He liked the style and the color more than her former bleach blonde locks. The style made her look more mature, more feminine.

"Savvy," he whispered, "I'd rather take you back…" He pulled her close and right there in the middle of downtown Fairplay, kissed her for the whole town to see. He pulled away and chuckled when Maggie's little hands reached up between them.

Smiling, he looked down at Savannah and noticed that her blue eyes were cloudy and unfocused, which made him smile even more.

"Come on, let's get the surprise over with so I can take my two ladies back home." She blinked a few times and then turned and started walking towards Holly's.

When he stepped in the front door of the newly remodeled place, he was surprised to see how well the place had turned out. If he didn't know any better, he would have thought he'd just stepped into a coffeehouse in downtown New York.

There were a few customers sitting around the front tables drinking coffee and enjoying baked goods.

"Here," she said and tugged him towards the far corner, near the fireplace. He noticed a group of people including Travis and Holly and a few other people he knew. When they approached, Travis stood and shook his hand.

"Good to have you back." He patted him on the arm and then Corey shook his hand, followed by a few of his other close friends. Maggie was taken from his arms and a beer was shoved in his hands.

When he finally sat down next to Savannah, he set his beer down untouched and reached for his daughter again.

"Thanks." He smiled over at her.

She tilted her head and looked at him in question. "For what?"

He chuckled. "For this. It's good to see everyone again." He nodded to the group of people who were easily the loudest group in the place.

She frowned a little. "Don't thank me. I mentioned that you were coming home the other day when we were here for play time and the next thing I know, Holly had put it all together," she whispered as she leaned closer to him. He got a quick whiff of her scent and instantly the desire for her was back full force.

"Do you think they'd mind if we left now?" He smiled and brushed a strand of her hair away from her face. He hadn't expected to see her frown and bite her bottom lip.

"Billy," she started to say, but was interrupted by Travis.

"So, tell us all about your job." Travis leaned closer to them. "We heard you had a bunch of protesters up there at one point."

Billy sighed and leaned away from Savannah. "Yeah, it's funny, the news said they were peaceful, but shooting a few dozen holes in our generators and destroying a few thousand dollars of equipment doesn't seem peaceful to me."

Everyone listened as he talked about the last six months. Then he turned the tables and smiled at Travis.

"Heard you popped the big question." He nodded towards Holly.

Travis laughed. "Yeah, we figure we'll get married this fall when her mother we'll be in town."

Billy shook his head. "Dropping like flies around here."

Travis laughed. "Everyone except Corey there." He nodded to their friend who was busy flirting with April behind the bar.

"Corey?" Billy smiled at his friend. "Corey is a habitual flirt. It'll take a miracle to get him to settle down. He smiled bigger when his friend started walking back to the table. "Besides," he said a little louder, "who would want someone so ugly."

Corey laughed. "You shouldn't talk about yourself like that. Besides, everyone knows you've already gotten yourself a woman." Then he laughed. "Well, two of them now." He nodded to the sleeping baby that Holly was holding.

His smile wavered a little as he looked over at Savannah, who was looking like she'd rather be anywhere but sitting in this room full of old friends.

Chapter Seven

Savannah tried not to let her nerves show. Everyone was too busy chatting and joking with each other to pay her any real attention.

In the last six months, she'd done a lot of thinking and soul searching. She'd enjoyed the time she spent with Tracy and Carmen, even though she still didn't consider them close friends. She thought that their friendships were not only helping her, but them as well.

But at this point in her life, all she knew for a fact was that no one was going to come between her and Maggie.

As she watched Billy with his friends, she wondered how she'd gotten into this whole mess in the first place. Sure, Billy was a good friend. Actually, he was one of the only guys in town she had always deemed just a friend.

He'd been there during her long on-again, off-again relationship with Travis. She glanced over at Travis now and saw him reach under the table and take Holly's hand in his own. She had to admit, the pair looked good together, like they were really in love. It was strange. She would have never pegged Holly as Travis' type. But she'd gotten to know and understand Holly over the last few months and could see why the two of them were good for one another.

She supposed Billy wasn't really her type ether, yet they had ended up sleeping together. She glanced next to her and tried to hide the fact that she was studying him. But it wasn't as if they were together, together. She had to admit, he had always been very sexy.

He had a nice side profile. His nose was straight and he had a strong looking chin. But what really set him aside were his dark eyes and jet-black hair. She knew it was rich and thick under her fingers, and she had loved running her hands through it.

Shaking her head, she blinked and tried to focus on the conversations around her. Maggie had fallen asleep in Holly's arms and she desperately wished for the shield of her daughter in her lap.

Then Billy reached over and took her hand and she forgot about everything else. His hands were warm and strong. There were a few rough spots along his palm, but she didn't mind.

She couldn't remember how they had felt against her skin. In all honesty, she couldn't really remember much about the few times they'd gotten together.

Glancing over at him, she frowned a little as he smiled at her. She knew that most people in town were expecting them to be together once he returned to town, but honestly, she didn't know what was going to happen. Only that she was living at his place and she wasn't willing to give up any time with her daughter, even a minute.

She'd had a few friends in high school whose parents were divorced. She knew that they had spent their childhood being ushered from one parent to the other. She glanced over at her daughter again. No matter what, she wouldn't want that for her daughter. But she wasn't sure she wanted to be with Billy full-time. After all, she didn't really know him.

By the time everyone was starting to leave, her stomach was in knots. She wished the decision would be taken out of her hands. Her parents hadn't been much help in the last few months. All they talked to her about was how well Billy was doing and how nice it would be for him to return.

"Everything okay?" Billy asked as he shifted Maggie's sleeping body into his arms.

She looked over at him and tried to smile. "Sure." She almost missed a step as they walked back towards the house.

He chuckled. "Really? Because it looks like you're about to jump out of your skin."

She frowned at him. One thing she'd always prided herself in was the fact that she could hide her emotions well. She'd been the talk of the town for as long as she could remember, and ever since her party on her sixteenth birthday, she'd hid what was inside her from everyone else.

Pushing her shoulders back, she pasted on her "everything's fine" smile and nodded. "I was just thinking about something else." She pushed her hair behind her ear and started walking faster.

Billy took her hand and stopped her, turning her around. "I know this probably isn't what you had planned." She waited and watched him. "You know, between us."

Her eyes darted around. This was not the place she wanted to have this conversation, nor was it the time. Shrugging her shoulders, she started walking again, this time more quickly. "It's funny how life changes." She looked over her shoulder and was glad when she noticed him following her. "Sometimes things don't work out the way you planned. If you can't adapt, then life is going to suck." She smiled and hoped that would be the last of the conversation.

He was quiet the rest of the walk to the small house. She unlocked the door and he disappeared into Maggie's room, no doubt laying her down so she could finish her nap. Savannah knew that it wouldn't last much longer and smiled when she heard her start to fuss from the next room. Walking in, she saw him standing by the window, rocking Maggie in his arms.

When he heard her, he turned and smiled. "Looks like she doesn't like to be set down."

"She's probably wet." She walked over and held out her arms, but he shocked her by shaking his head.

"No, I'll take care of it." He stepped over to the changing table and laid her down.

This was going to be interesting. She remembered the first time he'd changed Maggie's diapers and cringed. Walking over, she sat down in the rocker and watched the show.

Maggie, for her part did, everything possible to make the situation go badly, even peeing on Billy when he'd finally managed to get her clean and powdered.

Savannah laughed as Billy cursed under his breath and started the whole process over again. "You're not making this any easier," he said over his shoulder.

"Oh, was I supposed to?" She smiled and watched him fumble with the sticky strips of the diapers.

He didn't answer since he was too busy trying to hold wiggly Maggie down.

"She likes to be naked." She laughed when her daughter flipped over again.

He looked over his shoulder while his hand held Maggie on the table. "If I remember right, so does her mother." His smirk caused her heart rate to spike. He'd never done that before. She frowned at his back as he continued to fumble with their daughter.

Her eyes ran over his wide shoulders and she felt something stir inside her. His hips were narrow and his butt looked absolutely delicious in his worn jeans. His brown work boots were dusty and even his faded blue shirt was making him look rugged and sexy, something she would have never said about Billy before.

Then again, she'd gone over a year without sex and the last person she'd actually slept with was standing across the room from her. Just that thought caused her heart to skip a beat.

She felt her hands shake and quickly shoved them under her legs. Her eyes watched his every move as he gently dressed their daughter again. He was chatting to her about all sorts of things and she hadn't even really been paying attention to what he was saying.

Closing her eyes, she tried desperately to get

her emotions under control again. She hated that pregnancy had cause so many emotions to flood to the surface. She just couldn't get a handle on why she was so nervous around him all of a sudden.

"If you're tired, you can go lay down. I'll take this shift." When she opened her eyes, Billy was standing over her with Maggie on his hip. Maggie was running her little hands over his chin and jabbering.

She smiled and shook her head. "No, I was just thinking." She moved to stand up. "Would you like some dinner?"

He stepped back so she could stand next to him and nodded. "I haven't had a home-cooked meal in months," he said, following her out of the room.

"Didn't you cook while you were away?" she asked, taking her apron off the hook and wrapping it around her waist.

"Sure, but I'm not very good at it." He smiled at her and shifted Maggie on his hip.

They looked good together. Maggie's hair had lightened up a lot to where it had a few highlights of blonde throughout it. They had matching eyes and grins and when Maggie laughed, she could hear Billy's laughter match hers. She wondered if him being back was going to be a good thing. After all, she and Maggie had gotten used to being alone around the small place.

She knew there was still gossip going around

town about her and Billy, especially with the younger crowd. Most everyone her age and older knew about his job, and that he was back in town.

She glanced over at Billy and Maggie again and smiled when she saw that he'd pulled the little girl up to his face and was giving her kisses on her tummy. His lips made funny noises as Maggie giggled and yanked on his hair.

Her mind flashed to an image of his lips running down her ribs, towards her lower belly, her fingers gripping his hair as he pleased her.

He glanced up at her and when their eyes connected, she felt her face flush with her inner thoughts. He stilled and his smile grew as he looked at her. She could see heat flood his eyes and, from across the small room, she felt herself heat even more.

Turning, she blocked the thoughts of Billy touching her from her mind as she pulled out the makings for fried chicken. She tried to busy herself, but every time she looked, he was watching her.

Billy couldn't keep his eyes off of Savannah. Not only was the dance of cooking exciting, the little white apron she'd tied around her waist had caused her clothes to hug her curves. She'd gained her sexy hourglass figure back and he couldn't stop himself from watching her backside as she dropped the chicken into the hot oil.

"Ouch." She jumped back a little and held her finger. He sat Maggie down in the playpen that sat just inside the living room door and rushed over to take Savannah's hand. She was running her left hand under cold water in the sink, and he pulled her hand up to look at it. A nasty white welt had started on the backside of two fingers.

"Here." He held her hand up. "Let me see." He pulled her closer to the back kitchen window so the light would stream over her hand. Then he used the dish towel to softly start wiping the water from the welts.

Reaching back, he pulled out a packet of burn cream from the medicine cabinet.

"I can—" she started, only to be shushed by him as he ripped open the small packet and began dabbing the white cream on the burns.

"My chicken is burning." She frowned at him.

He reached over, still holding her hand in his, and removed the pan from the burner. Then he went back to gently rubbing the cream over her two fingers.

"You should wear gloves when you fry foods." He frowned at the welts and knew they would blister and could leave tiny scars.

She shook her head. "I don't usually drop the

chicken in that quickly. But you were distracting me." She frowned as he pulled out a box of Band-Aids. "I can do this myself," she said, still frowning at him.

He shook his head. "I don't mind." He took two Band-Aids out and carefully put them on her fingers. "There." He smiled down at her. "Now, what's this about me distracting you?" He made sure to keep her close and he noticed her eyes heat when he backed her into the cabinet.

Her breath hitched and he saw her beautiful chest move with each labored breath.

"I…" she said, but then her eyes moved down to his lips and she shook her head a little. Her tongue darted out to lick her bottom lip and he felt like groaning. She'd worn soft pink lip gloss, something he'd never seen her wear before. Her usual style was dark lipstick. He liked the softer look and wondered if her lips would taste as good as they looked.

Using just his fingers, he nudged her until her hips were up against his. He watched her eyes open in shock as she felt his desire next to her stomach. He couldn't help it; he smiled a little more.

When he slowly dipped his head for a taste, he watched her eyes for any sign of denial, but all he saw was heat and uncertainty.

When their lips touched, he did groan. They

were softer than they looked, and he couldn't stop himself from exploring their softness. She tasted like strawberries and cream. His hands moved to her soft hair and tilted her head so he could get a better taste.

Her fingers gripped his shirt and when he pulled her closer, they wrapped around his shoulders and held on as he took her mouth more quickly. He hadn't planned on pushing her this quickly, but after just one taste, he'd had to have more.

Hoisting her onto the edge of the countertop, he moved between her legs, her core next to his desire, which was pushing up against the zipper of his jeans and wanting out. Wanting into the softness that he knew would be hot and ready for him.

When her fingers went into his hair, he felt her wince at the pain from the burn. He leaned back with concern in his eyes.

"Are you okay?" He looked into her soft eyes and watched her blink a few times until they were clear.

She nodded and licked her lips again and he closed his eyes. Resting his forehead against hers, he realized that Maggie was crying in the background. "Later." He pulled back and looked her in the eyes until she finally nodded. Then he helped her down off the countertop and made sure she was steady on her feet.

"Be more careful dropping the chicken in."

She nodded again.

"I'll go take care of Maggie." He smiled when she just nodded again. He liked knowing he could make her speechless.

He walked into the living room and looked down at his daughter, who was standing up inside her crib, crying. When she saw him, the tears stopped and she held her little hands up for him to pick her up.

He smiled. "Oh, no." He shook his head. "I can only spoil one of my girls at a time." He sat next to the crib and picked up the stuffed frog she'd dropped outside her crib. "Besides, I've heard that if I give in now, you will associate crying with getting what you want." He chuckled when she pouted as she realized he wasn't going to pick her up.

He could hear Savannah in the kitchen cooking again and thought about how he wanted to spoil her later that night. Then shaking his head clear, he distracted Maggie by making her frog dance around until Savannah called him in for dinner.

Chapter Eight

Savannah took her time feeding Maggie. Billy had retreated to the bedroom, claiming he needed a shower. She could hear the water running in the next room and felt her nerves jump.

Maggie reached up with her tiny fingers and touched her face as she ate. She enjoyed breast-feeding and had never thought that such a simple act could bind her and her daughter so closely.

She had bottles, pumps, and even formula, but she wouldn't take away a moment of the time she spent each day holding her daughter, knowing that what she was giving her was the best thing for her.

"What do you think of your daddy?" she whispered, brushing Maggie's soft hair away from her chubby face.

Her daughter's eyes opened and looked around when she heard the word "Daddy," causing Savannah to smile. "Yeah, I'm kind of glad he's back, too." She watched her daughter's eyes close again and knew that this time her daughter would stay asleep.

Leaning her head back, she closed her eyes and thought of what waited for her in the next room. She was nervous. The changes in her body were part of the cause, but the changes between her and Billy were part of it as well.

It was funny. Sex was something she used to do a lot and she'd always enjoyed it. But now, after over a year of not having someone touch her, she felt like a virgin all over again. No, that wasn't right. Even when she'd been untouched by someone she'd wanted to touch her, she'd never felt like this before. Never.

She heard a noise and opened her eyes to see Billy standing in the doorway, looking at her. She glanced down and saw that Maggie's little head had fallen away from her breast in sleep. She moved her shirt back into place and started lifting her sleeping daughter.

"Here," he said quietly and rushed over to

gently pick up the baby. "I'll take her."

She nodded and watched him carry Maggie over to the crib. He stood there holding their sleeping girl for a moment. Then glanced over his shoulder at her.

"Are you supposed to lay her on her stomach or something?" He frowned.

She smiled and walked over to show him how Maggie liked to sleep. She patted her daughter a few times on the back until, in sleep, she burped and settled down with her frog blanket and a smile on her lips.

"Frogs?" He shook his head and smiled.

She smiled as they looked down at the sleeping baby. "Frogs."

He wrapped an arm around her shoulders and pulled her close. "She is perfect, isn't she?" He placed a kiss on the top of her head and she felt her heart skip.

Her throat had closed again and all she could do was nod her head.

Then he pulled her with him as he walked out of the room. Holding her hand, he turned her around just outside their door and pulled her up against the wall. His mouth was over hers quickly, and she felt her breath hitch as his hands roamed over her sides.

"I've waited." He shook his head and pulled

back a little. "Waited too long." His eyes closed as he rested his forehead on hers. "Don't make me wait any longer, Savvy." She heard his voice crack.

Shaking her head, she said, "No, no more waiting." Then she pulled his head back down to hers until his lips took hers and all of her nerves melted away with his warm lips.

When his hands started tugging on her shirt, she stiffened for just a moment until his mouth traveled down her neck. She rested her head back against the door and closed her eyes to the pure enjoyment of being touched again.

Then she was tugging and pulling on his shirt and walking backwards into the small bedroom. He followed her and shut the door with his foot as he helped pull his shirt off.

When she saw his tan shoulders and stomach finally exposed for her view, she melted even more. Why hadn't she noticed during their Skype sessions that he'd gotten so muscular over the last six months?

She ran her fingers over his tight skin slowly and smiled as he flexed under her light touch. "Someone else has been working out." She smiled and wrapped her arms around his shoulders.

He nodded and smiled. "And now that I've shown you mine…" His fingers played under her shirt and started to lift it up slowly.

Her smile faltered for a split second before she

closed her eyes and let him lift it up and over her head. He heard his breath hitch and her eyes flew open to see the heat as he looked at her.

"Beautiful," he whispered as he ran his finger over her collarbone then down over the mound of her breast.

She sighed and leaned back, letting her head fall back once more.

"I've dreamed of touching you again," he said, just before his mouth continued the trail down her neck as his fingers played over her heated skin. "Dreamed of tasting you." He used his fingers and pulled her nursing bra aside. For a split second, she froze, remembering that she was wearing the ugly white thing instead of something lacy and sexy.

"Don't," he said, realizing her thought. "It's perfect. You're perfect." He pulled the material aside and exposed her. Then his smile grew. "Perfect," he said again.

When his fingers and lips went back to her skin, she forgot all about her awkward undergarments. Instead, she found herself tugging on his jeans and wishing he would go faster.

"Easy," he chuckled. "I've waited a long time to have you like this again." He pulled back and she felt like growling.

Shaking her head, she bit her bottom lip. "I need it now." Her eyes traveled up and down him. He stood in front of her in nothing but his boxers now, and she thought that he looked just like the underwear ads she'd seen on the back covers of the magazines down at the Grocery Stop.

His tan skin was tight over every cord, every muscle that ran along his ribs, his stomach, his arms. Everything was better than she remembered. The feel of warm skin over hard muscle. The taste of his mouth on hers. The smell of man. She'd missed it all. How had she let herself go this long without it? Why had she?

Then his fingers touched her sides and she remembered the long white stretch marks that ran along that path. She reached over and flipped off the lights, sending the room into total darkness.

She heard him chuckle, then the lights flooded the room again.

"You're not getting off that easy." He smiled.

She frowned and flipped the switch off again. She heard him chuckle once more, and then he left her side. Her hands dropped by her side, and she stood in the dark wondering what he was doing. The light beside the bed flipped on and she saw him standing across the room. She started to think of how she could convince him to flip it off as well.

He crossed his arms over his chest and shook his head when she started to move towards it. "It stays on." Something told her that pouting wouldn't work with him this time.

116

She'd lost all control of the situation and for the first time in her life, she knew without a doubt that she was going to enjoy every second of the rest of her evening.

Billy couldn't stop smiling as Savannah stood across the room in nothing but a white cotton bra and her black leggings. She'd removed the sexy boots at the front door and he found her bright pink toenails sexier than hell.

Just being this close to a woman again was sending his body into overdrive. Knowing it was Savannah, the mother of his child, the woman he'd been in love with for as long as he could remember, was like adding nitro to his system, pushing his body to want her faster.

He shook his head and dropped his arms to his side. Her eyes were traveling over him, and he could see the heat in them as she enjoyed what she looked at.

Working on the pipeline had been hard work, but during his off hours, he'd done some lifting with a weight set the guys had in the trailer. Not that he was vain, but he'd gained a few extra pounds since graduating from high school. He'd also started getting a beer gut like the one he'd always hated on his father.

Glancing down at himself, he smiled a little. Gone was the beer gut and in its place was a well-toned six-pack. It wasn't as impressive as the abs on some of the guys that worked on his crew, but he felt he could hold his own and knew how hard he'd worked for it.

"So?" He looked back up at her.

Her eyes darted to his in question.

"Are you going to come over here and let me enjoy every inch of your body?"

Her face flushed, and then her shoulders went back in a classic Savannah move, and she marched across the room. He would have laughed if seeing her coming toward him hadn't turned him on more.

When she reached him, she took his head into her hands and leaned up to kiss him, but he pulled back and put his hands on her shoulders. "Let me." He smiled when he saw her frown. "Savvy. I want to enjoy looking at you." When her frown increased, he chuckled. "You have a beautiful body." He ran the back of his fingers down her ribs and her breath caught. "So beautiful."

Her eyes were closed now and she shook her head from side to side.

"I have stretch marks." It came out as a whisper.

Reaching up, he put a finger under her chin

until she opened her eyes and looked deep into his. "If you do, trust me, I don't see them or care. All I see is perfection."

Her frown wavered, so he continued to tell her exactly what he did see. Her breasts were perfect, full and supple. Ripe for his mouth. He reached around and unclasped the bra and slowly drew it down and off her shoulders.

She tried to reach out and cover herself, but he took her hands and held them aside. "Perfection," he whispered as he looked at her. "They're perfect for feeding our baby, and perfect for this." He leaned his head down and started running his mouth over her exposed skin. "They're soft, yet strong enough to stand up to the daily feedings of a six-month-old." He looked up at her and noticed that her eyes were unfocused as she looked down at him, so he continued his exploration.

He ran a finger lightly over her flat stomach. He noticed small white stretch marks, but could only see the beauty in them. "It's amazing how your body grew and held our child in here, nurturing and protecting her. And now you're so small, so perfect." He ran his mouth over every soft inch of her skin. Her fingers were in his hair, pulling and pushing as she enjoyed his movements. He enjoyed the sounds she made as he pleased her. His hands went to her hips and he slowly moved the black cotton over her narrow hips. "But I think my favorite part is this." He took her bare hips in his hands and pulled her closer to him. "The fact that your hips are now smaller than ever." He smiled and laid his head against her stomach as he ran his hands up and down her hips and thighs. "I've always been a butt man." He chuckled with her as his hands gripped her backside. "I know, I know. Every man in town thinks I'm crazy." He looked up at her as she shook her head.

"You're killing me." Her frown fell away. "Take me to bed."

He chuckled. "I like torturing you." He turned his head into her softness again and ran his mouth over her flat hips until he reached the soft white cotton that shielded her from his further exploration. Dipping his finger underneath, he pulled the cotton down her smooth legs and ran his hands up and down the toned muscles in each leg.

His eyes went to her sex and his mouth actually watered. When she was free of all clothing, she tried to move back towards the bed and she reached for the light. He chuckled and took her hands in his, holding her still. She groaned and tried to put up a little fight, and he gripped both of her hands behind her back with one of his.

"No," he growled. "I'll have you my way." He knelt between her legs and with his free hand pushed her legs wider. He heard her curse at him as his mouth took her sex. He used his tongue on her until her curses were replaced with moans and panting.

She pulled at her hands behind her back and so

120

he released them. They moved up and dug deep into his hair and pulled his head closer to her as he pleased her.

She moved one of her legs up to the edge of the bed, exposing herself more for him. His fingers dug into her hips as he enjoyed her, and when he felt like he couldn't hold back any more, he pushed her back onto the bed and moved above her.

"I can't believe how much I want you." He rained kisses along her jaw as he slipped inside her slowly and knew without a doubt that he was where he belonged. That they were made for one another.

As he looked down at her soft hair fanned out on his pillowcases, he felt a little overwhelmed. She was more beautiful than he remembered, than he had ever imagined in his memories.

"Savvy," he groaned as her blue eyes slid open and looked up at him with want. Her nails dug into his shoulders as she pulled him closer.

When her shoulders moved off the mattress, he wrapped his arms around her, holding on until he thought he might cut off her air supply.

"Billy, hurry," she moaned and he was a slave to her desires. Pulling back, he used his hips and watched as she threw her head back and squeezed her eyes tight.

He'd always enjoyed watching her lose herself, but this time was different. This time he knew it was the first of many. When they'd been together in the past, he'd never thought that he would get to experience it again.

He smiled at her as he felt her settle down underneath him. He was going to make sure that this was just the first in a lifetime of pleasures he would bring for her.

"Billy?" She looked up at him, shaking him from his deep thoughts, and he realized he'd yet to have his physical release. Shaking his head and chuckling lightly, he leaned down and started kissing her.

"Soon." He deepened the kisses and felt her building up again underneath him. Her legs wrapped around his hips and her hips moved with his. "More," he growled, feeling himself building higher.

Then she shocked him by pushing on his shoulder until she reversed their positions. She smiled down at him and pushed her hair away from her eyes.

"I think it's time you let me take the reins." Her smile grew as her hips started rotating. He tried to keep his eyes glued to her beauty, hovering above him, but the pleasure she was causing was so great and he felt the brightness of it consuming him.

Closing his eyes, he dug his fingers into her soft hips and cried out her name as she took everything he'd ever held for her, in one quick moment.

Chapter Nine

She lay there and listened to Billy's heartbeat slow down. She'd never imaged it would be like this. Her chest actually hurt.

In all her years, she'd never allowed herself to get this close to anyone before. Not even Travis, whom she'd been with the longest. True, she'd been mad at him when he'd proposed to Alexis West, but she'd known it wouldn't last. After all, the week after he'd gotten engaged to her, he'd crawled through her window.

Now, as she lay here and listened to Billy sleep lightly below her, she doubted Travis would ever cheat on Holly. Nor would Savannah allow him to crawl in her window anymore. He was different. She was different.

Sighing, she snuggled closer to Billy's warm chest. She didn't know if she wanted to be with Billy for the rest of her life, but at least he was kind to her and to Maggie, and that was the most important thing to her right now. Not to mention that she had really enjoyed the sex they'd just had.

She smiled into his chest and let her eyes close shut. She drifted off to the sound of his heart and the memory of how much pleasure she'd gotten from him.

She woke around one and heard Maggie crying from the monitor on the nightstand. She could tell from the pressure in her chest that it was feeding time again.

She was halfway across the room when she realized she was still very naked. Grabbing her robe from the hook on the back of the door, she wrapped it around herself and glanced back at the bed.

Billy sat up in the bed, smiling at her.

"I was wondering if you were going to march around the house like that. Not that I was complaining." His smile grew.

Her eyes narrowed as she watched him get out of bed, gloriously naked. She had to blink a few times for her eyes to finally focus on his face. His smile was huge.

"I'll go get her." He started to pull on his boxers.

She shook her head. "No, I need to feed her."

He frowned a little. "What about a bottle?"

She chuckled. "Trust me. This time, it's all me." She turned, only to be stopped by his hand on her shoulder.

"Savvy, I want to help out." He frowned down at her.

Her eyebrows shot up. "It's not that." She sighed, feeling slightly embarrassed. She could feel her body reacting to the crying baby and if he didn't let her go to her daughter soon, the front of her robe would be soaked. "I *need* to feed her." She stretched out the word, hoping he'd get her meaning. When he just looked at her blankly, she sighed and closed her eyes. "Billy, if you don't let me go, I'll burst with milk."

She felt his hands tighten briefly on her shoulders, and then they dropped away. "Sorry," he mumbled and she quickly turned around and rushed out.

Gathering up Maggie, she settled down as the girl started sucking hungrily.

She was shocked when she heard Billy walk into the baby's room.

"Does she wake you up every night?"

She looked up at him and nodded. His frown

grew.

"What about cutting back a little, you know, with the bottle."

She shrugged her shoulders. "I don't mind."

"Don't you need more sleep?" He walked over to her and watched their daughter as she ate.

Savannah shrugged her shoulder. "She'll go back down for a few more hours." She yawned and looked over at the frog clock on the wall. "Then she'll be up for good around six." She smiled. "That's when we usually go for our morning walk. Before it gets too hot."

His eyebrows shot up. "I'll go with you." He knelt down next to her. Maggie's little hand reached up and took his as he brushed her hair away from her face.

He chuckled. "She's got a good grip." Then his eyes softened as he watched her eat. "And an appetite."

Savannah laughed.

By the time they made it back to their bed, Maggie was asleep again.

"Does she eat from the bottle every now and then?" he asked, pulling off his shorts and crawling into the bed. She was so breathless at seeing him naked, she almost forgot what he'd asked her.

"Yes." It came out as a whisper. "I pump

sometimes and sometimes I give her formula."

He nodded. "Are you going to crawl back in here? Or did you plan on sleeping standing up?" He smiled as he held the blanket open for her to crawl in.

She was standing at the side of the bed, her robe tucked tightly around her. She thought for a quick moment about grabbing a pair of her pajamas, but he shook his head when he saw her eyes dart over to the dresser.

"Savvy, come back to bed." His voice was low and she felt a wave of heat rush through her body.

She undid the tie to her robe and his eyes traveled up and down her body when she pulled the cotton from her shoulders. She stood for a moment next to the bed, frozen under his gaze. Then he reached for her and she went down to him, knowing that she wouldn't get the few extra hours of sleep and knowing that she didn't care.

Billy waved to some people across the street as he pushed Maggie's stroller down the sidewalk. The sun was already up, since they'd gotten a slower start this morning.

It had been almost a week since he'd gotten back home, and he was already settling into the new schedule. He enjoyed the daily walks that they took as a family, even though the first one was usually before the sun was up. He'd always been a late sleeper. When work demanded that he be up earlier, it usually took a few cups of coffee before he felt alive. But now all it took was hearing the giggles of his daughter first thing in the morning.

He looked down at Maggie, sitting up in her stroller. Her dark eyes, which almost matched his perfectly, traveled all over, taking in everything.

"She's smart," he blurted out and winced when he realized how stupid he sounded.

Savannah glanced over at him and nodded. She was wearing a light blue wind jacket with tight, dark blue yoga pants. The white top she wore underneath the jacket clung to her and he'd wished she hadn't zipped the jacket up all the way.

"Yes, I've noticed it as well. She takes in everything."

He smiled. "Exactly." He nodded and continued to look down at his daughter. "I was watching the other kids yesterday at the park and none of the other kids looked around like she does.

"Like she's trying to understand everything." Savannah smiled. "I was thinking it was just me. You know, everyone says that parents think the best of their kids, but in this case…"

"Yeah." He sighed. "What would you say to a night out with me?" he blurted out.

Savannah stopped walking and he had to

quickly pull the stroller to a stop. He glanced over his shoulder at Savannah in question. Her head was tilted and she was biting her bottom lip.

"Like a date?"

He thought about it. "Well, sure. I thought we'd go into Tyler for dinner. Maybe a show."

She blinked a few times and he was starting to feel a little strange standing on the sidewalk waiting for an answer.

"I guess my folks can watch Maggie for a few hours."

His smile was quick. "How about Friday?"

She started walking slowly again. "I'll call them."

"Will you be okay? Being away from her like that." He nodded towards her chest, causing her to frown.

"I'll have to pump beforehand." She frowned a little. "As long as we aren't out too late." She smiled.

As they walked the rest of the mile and half back to their house, his mind raced with options. He'd never really taken a girl out on a date before. There had been plenty of girls before, but he'd never taken any out on an actual date.

His steps faltered when he realized he didn't know of a good place in Tyler to take a woman.

He knew of over two dozen bars and hole-in-the-wall dance places, but nothing came to mind that would be suitable for an evening out with the mother of his child.

When they turned the last corner and the green house came into sight, he realized he knew exactly who to ask. He was happily surprised to see her old truck parked in front of the diner at the end of the block.

"Um…" He stopped and waited for Savannah to turn to him. "I need to stop in at the diner for a moment." He pushed Maggie's stroller a little until Savannah took it. "I'll be right back. Then we can have some breakfast."

"Why don't we go with you and have breakfast at Mama's instead?"

He stopped. "Are you allowed back in there?" He coughed when she glared at him. "I mean, sure. That would be great." How was he going to get Alex alone to ask her about a good place to go in Tyler?

"Maggie likes Mama's." Savannah chatted as they walked the block and a half to the diner.

When they walked in, he was expecting the crowded room to hush as they noticed Savannah walk in, but instead, people waved and said hello to them.

The last time he'd been in town, she'd been banned from Mama's due to a slight misunderstanding between her and Jamella.

But as they found their way across the large room, which had recently been remodeled, he was surprised to watch the owner of the diner rush across the room and pluck Maggie right out of her stroller.

"Der's my girl." Jamella kissed his daughter's chubby cheeks to Maggie's delight. His daughter's high squeal and laughter filled the room. Several people looked over and chuckled. "Well, it'n about time you'd show'd up again." Jamella smiled down at him, moving Maggie to her hip.

"Yes, ma'am. It's good to be back." He set down his menu.

Jamella nodded. "You're back for a while?"

He nodded. "I start my two week shift in three weeks."

She nodded and looked down at Maggie. "I'm stealing dis child o' yours for a while." She chuckled when Maggie grabbed at her big necklace. "Got to show my godchild off." She glanced at them and glared a little. "Dat is if'n you two ever get around to making it official..." She let out a humf and then walked away with their daughter.

He leaned across the booth and whispered, since everyone in town knew that Jamella had hearing like an elephant. "What was that all about?"

Savannah shrugged her shoulders. "She and the town sheriff think that they should be Maggie's godparents."

He smiled. "I don't see why not. After all, aren't they yours?"

She glanced up at him. "Sheriff Miller is my godfather, yes."

He nodded. "And since the sheriff and Jamella are an item…"

She shrugged and looked back down at her menu, but he saw her eyes dart across the room where Jamella was showing off Maggie to everyone she could. He watched a small smile form on her lips and couldn't help but smile himself.

"Then it's settled." He set his menu down.

"What?" She set her menu down and sat back as Alex walked over and set two glasses of water down in front of them.

"I can't believe how fast she's growing." Alex smiled, looking off towards Jamella and Maggie.

He watched Savannah's face for any sign of dislike, which he'd seen every time she'd dealt with Alex before. But this time, the only thing on her face was a questioning look about his earlier statement.

When Alex looked back down at them, she nodded. "I'll give you two some time to think about what you want."

He had a funny feeling that she understood they wanted to be left alone for a moment.

"What's settled?" Savannah frowned.

He reached over and took her hand. "Jamella and the sheriff will be Maggie's godparents."

She frowned even more. "But…" She shook her head, then leaned forward and whispered. "We aren't married."

He chuckled. "Why not?"

She sat back, her frown growing. "Why not, what?"

"Why not get married?" he said clearly.

She jerked her hand away from him and frowned. Shaking her head, she picked up her menu again and he cursed Mama's new bigger menus, since he couldn't see her eyes over the top of it.

Reaching over, he pulled her menu down. "This is not the time." She looked around and he could see that several people near them had overheard their conversation and were watching and waiting for her response. "Or the place to discuss something like this," she hissed out quietly.

He felt like a heel all of a sudden. She was right. Looking around the diner, he realized that a room full of people that knew both of their pasts all too well wasn't the right place. But he had no problem with the time. After all, they did have a child together and had been getting along wonderfully since he'd returned home.

He enjoyed the time he'd spent with her during the day, but the time they spent at night in bed was the best. He nodded and picked up his menu again just as Jamella returned with Maggie.

"I'd better get back to it." She sighed and handed him his daughter, but not before placing several kisses on her cheek. "Now, it'n about time you two had a night out." She frowned down at them. "After all, if'n you're only goin' to be in town for another week or so." She shook her head. "Two weeks here, two gone." She turned to Alex who was walking towards them to get their order. "Girl, where did you say dat man of yours took you last time?"

Alex stopped and looked at Jamella. "Where? Oh, Antonio's Bistro. Some of the best Italian food in Texas. It's just past the mall, can't miss it."

Billy wondered if his thoughts were written somewhere on his face. Then Jamella smiled. "If'n you need a baby sitter…" She smiled, then laughed when Maggie tugged on Billy's face and took all his attention for the next few minutes as he tried to order his breakfast.

Chapter Ten

Savannah tried not to let her anger show during the rest of breakfast. She pasted on one of her "everything's fine" smiles even though she was boiling on the inside.

How dare Billy embarrass her like that. Especially at Mama's. It had only been a few months since the sheriff had hinted that Jamella would allow her back into the place. And now Billy was making a big scene for everyone to hear.

He couldn't believe he'd blurted that out about marriage, and she'd stewed all through breakfast. Now, as they walked back towards the house, she remained silent and wished more than anything

135

that she was back at home so she could lock herself in her room for the rest of the day instead of having the blow up she knew was building.

When they walked in the door, she grabbed up Maggie, who looked more tired than she usually looked after their morning walks. It was probably all the excitement at the diner that had her daughter nodding off as she laid her in her crib.

She desperately wished for a reason to stay in her daughter's room, but she knew that she needed the sleep. Shutting the door quietly, she walked into the kitchen to get a glass of water.

After filling up a glass, she turned and bumped into something solid, spilling the water all over her workout shirt.

"Sorry." Billy chuckled and reached for a hand towel. When he started brushing it down her shirt, she yanked it from him and walked over to the sink to wipe her shirt herself.

Even though her back was to him, she could tell that he knew she wasn't pleased with him.

"I'm sorry about the water. I didn't know you were going to turn around," he said, and she could hear that he was right behind her.

She gritted her teeth and turned on him. "This place it too small for the three of us. I mean, every time I turn around…" She motioned towards him as he stood two feet away from her. She closed her eyes in frustration.

He stepped back a few feet until his shoulders hit the door frame. He crossed his arms over his chest as he watched her. "I'm sorry," he said again.

"Stop saying that." It came out as a scream. She marched to the front room, knowing it was the farthest they could get from Maggie's room. She wasn't surprised when she turned around to see Billy standing in the doorway watching her.

She growled and threw up her hands. "I need some time to myself. How am I supposed to get that in such a small place." She felt the room closing in on her and put her hand on the back of the sofa to steady herself.

"Savvy—"

"Don't Savvy me," she said loudly. "You just proposed to me at Mama's!" She felt her breath hitch. "At Mama's!" she screamed.

He shook his head. "I—" She held up her hand to stop him.

"Don't! I don't want to hear it."

He started to walk towards her with his hands out, but she quickly picked up the little glass bowl she'd always set her keys in and tossed it at his head. He easily ducked, and when it shattered against the back wall of the room, she heard Maggie start to cry.

She groaned and threw up her hands. Then she turned and grabbed her jacket again and yelled over her shoulder as she walked out. "I'm going out for a walk."

She slammed the front door behind her, took a deep breath, and rested her head back against the door. She heard a noise and opened her eyes. She was horrified to see three people standing on the sidewalk in front of her house.

Mr. and Mrs. Cole stood talking to Sheriff Miller, who quickly started walking her way.

She groaned and wished she could go back inside, but she didn't want to face Billy just yet.

Grinding her back teeth, she straightened her shoulders and started marching down the sidewalk.

"Everything okay?" The sheriff looked between her and the house.

"Everything's just fine," she said quickly and continued to walk away.

"Well, it's just…" The sheriff kept up with her. When she looked, Mr. and Mrs. Cole were glancing at her from their driveway, concern in their eyes. "I was talking to Phil and Alice"—he nodded to her neighbors—"when we heard yelling and a crash."

She stopped and turned to him. "Nothing but a simple fight," she blurted out. What was she doing? She would have never admitted anything like that before. Private lives stayed private. She pushed her shoulders back further and turned on her heels. "Now, if everyone is done butting their noses into my personal life, I'm going for a long walk." She turned and headed away from the diner and the little green house as quickly as she could.

Fueled on anger, hurt, and embarrassment, her feet carried her as far as the outskirts of town. She turned down the old highway and stopped on the old rickety bridge that should have been torn down a dozen or so years back. It still looked strong, but most of its boards were too fragile to support a vehicle.

She'd come here a million times over the years. Even more recently for her visits with Tracy.

Sitting down on the side of the bridge, she let her legs hang over the edge as she tossed pebbles from the bridge into the calm water below her.

She knew she'd been childish with Billy. Closing her eyes, she rested her forehead on the rusted steel girder, much like Tracy always did.

The heat of the day had snuck up on her, and she felt sweat dripping down her back. Her breasts ached and she knew she was quickly approaching feeding time for Maggie. Soon, no matter what she did, they would become terribly painful and she would need her daughter. But she continued to sit on the bridge, looking over the edge at the water.

She was Savannah Douglas. She'd had so many plans for her life. She was going to find the richest man in Texas and marry him. He'd fly her in a private jet to Italy or Paris and propose to her at a fancy restaurant, getting down on his knee in the most expensive suit his money would buy, with the largest, most expensive ring he could find held out for her approval.

Rolling her shoulders, she looked up when she heard a bird chirp on a tree branch a few feet away from the calm shore of the water. It was bright red and it danced around next to a rather dull looking brown bird with a red beak. She watched the dance as the male cardinal chirped and jumped to prove his worthiness for the female. Laughing out loud, she watched the pair of birds fly off into the brush together.

"At least he danced for you," she called out to the happy pair.

"What's the matter? Didn't that son of mine show you a good time?"

She jumped and gasped as her hand flew to her chest. She felt her fingers tingle from fear as Billy Jackson Sr. walked towards her. The old wood boards creaked under his weight.

The last time she'd seen him, she'd still been in school. It was the week before he'd driven into Houston and gotten in a bar fight that had put him away for life, or so she'd thought.

Shaking her head, she blinked a few times. She must be imagining him. After all, he'd gotten life in prison. Right?

Then she heard him laugh. "No, sweetie pie, it's really me." He smiled and, for a moment, she could see Billy. Then his grin turned into something darker. She quickly got up and took a few steps back, glancing around her. She wished she hadn't taken a walk to some place so remote.

"What do you want?" She thought about running.

He laughed. "Oh, sweet thing, there's a lot that I want." He smiled again and stopped just a few feet away from her. His eyes traveled up and down her and, for the first time since losing all the baby weight, she wished she weighed more so she didn't feel him undressing her with his eyes. Her stomach started to roll.

She could see a lot of Billy in his looks—his dark hair, dark eyes, strong jaw—but the evil lying underneath his skin caused her to shiver with fear. She had always felt that way around him. She could always spot the creeps in a room, probably because of her experience with her uncle.

She straightened her shoulders and crossed her arms over her chest.

"Why are you here?" She took a step back and hated herself for the weakness.

He noticed her move and smiled. "Why, to see my grandchild."

"She's not here." She looked around and motioned with her hands. "Why did you follow me here?"

He chuckled. "I always knew you were a smart one. Like your old man." He tilted his worn straw hat back on his head and sighed. "I figured you could help your dear ol' father-in-law out, seeing as I've just gotten out of the slammer for good behavior." He chuckled again.

"What do you want?" she said again, grinding her back teeth again.

"Money. Plain and simple. Cash. I figured ten thousand ought to hold me over for a while." He winked at her.

She gasped. "You're joking?"

He shook his head and his smile fell away. "I know what your family is worth." Then his smile was back. "Besides, it would keep me too busy to show up to that pretty little green house of yours someday, letting nothing stop me from seeing my grandbaby."

His meaning was clear and she felt all her blood go cold. "I…" Her mouth gone dry. "I don't have my checkbook on me."

He laughed. "Well, I guess that's a good thing. I haven't opened up a checking account to cash a check just yet." He winked at her again. "I did say cash."

She nodded. "I…" She couldn't think.

"Well, that's all right, I understand." He dusted off his elbows from where he was leaning back against the old bridge. "I figured you would have to go to the bank. I'll be in town for another day. Why don't we just meet here again tomorrow." He looked down at his watch and nodded. "Same time?"

She glanced down at her watch and saw that it was a quarter past ten.

Before she could think it through, she nodded. She was relieved when he nodded and tipped his hat at her.

"I'll see you tomorrow." He started walking away, then turned around and said over his shoulder, "And Savannah, don't be late." His eyes were mean and she felt herself shiver in the heat of the day.

She waited until he hopped back into the old truck at the other end of the bridge—how hadn't she heard it arrive earlier?—before she started walking quickly back towards home.

By the time she arrived, it was ten past eleven. She was covered in sweat and was thankful that Billy was in Maggie's room. She could hear him talking to their daughter softly as he read her a book.

She walked into the bathroom, locked the door behind her, and stripped off her sweaty clothes. Setting the shower to cold, she stepped in and let the water cool her down so she could clear her mind.

Billy heard Savannah walk back into the house, but since he'd just gotten Maggie to finally settle down, he didn't move. It had taken him a half hour after Savannah left—and a crash course in making a bottle—to get her to settle down. It was obvious that she was tired, but she'd fussed at him until he'd found a book about the frog princess and started reading. Now, he kept reading to his daughter in a low voice until he felt her little head resting against his chest, and he was sure that she'd fallen to sleep. When he moved to lay her down, however, she jolted back up and looked at him. Then to his horror, she started screaming again.

"It's okay; Daddy's going to go talk to Mommy." He laid her down and stuck her little lip out in a pout. "No, no." He started to reach for her. "Don't cry."

He took another step towards her and heard the bedroom door open.

"If you constantly pick her up, she'll become spoiled," Savannah said from the doorway. She looked fresh in a pair of faded jeans and a clean white button up shirt. Her hair was still wet and she wasn't wearing any makeup. He'd seen her without makeup before, but now she had a light tan and her skin glowed, making her more attractive.

"What?" He turned all the way towards her.

She leaned against the door and frowned at him. Earlier, he hadn't known what had set her off. Then she'd mentioned the proposal and he'd finally caught up with her. Now, he felt like a complete fool for mentioning marriage in the diner.

"If you always pick her up when she's crying, she'll become spoiled and always cry to get what she wants." She turned and started to walk out of the room. He followed behind her and stood just inside Maggie's door, watching his daughter throw a bigger fit than Savannah had earlier.

"Yeah, but…" He turned towards Savannah, who walked over to him and shut the door, closing out his daughter's screams.

"Wait for it." She held up her finger and counted to five silently.

He didn't know how she knew it would happen, but around four, his daughter's screams turned silent.

Savannah took his hand and walked him into the kitchen where she took another glass from the cupboard.

One thing you could say about Billy, he was a fast learner. So, he stayed on the other side of the room as she drank the water and set the glass in the sink.

145

"I had a visit from your father." She turned and looked at him.

"What?" The words hit him like a brick. He rushed across the small room towards her. "Are you okay?" He took her shoulders into his hands.

She shrugged him off, but he held her still and looked into her eyes to see if he could judge her reaction.

"I'm fine. I can handle myself." She walked over and sat at the small kitchen table. He followed her lead and slowly sat down at the table. His fisted hands sat on the shiny wood.

"What happened?" he said between gritted teeth.

She sighed and told him how his father had followed her to the old bridge and basically threatened their daughter if she didn't give him ten grand.

As he listened to her story, he became even more agitated and stood up to pace the small room.

"Bastard," he growled out when she was done talking, causing her to jump a little. Then he turned on her. "I'll deal with him." He turned to leave and she jumped up from the table and grabbed his arm.

"Wait." She pulled on his arm until he stopped. "What exactly are you going to do? Pay him off?"

He stopped and looked down at her. She could probably see anger in his eyes, but he didn't care at this point.

"Hell, no. He won't get another dime of my money," he growled out.

She dropped her arm and looked at him like she'd been slapped. "Another?"

He shrugged his shoulders. "He contacted me a few weeks ago and got ten grand out of me. He shook his head. "But the game stops here." He turned to leave again. She rushed over and stepped in front of him.

"What do you plan on doing?"

He looked down at her. "He's my father. I'll take care of it." He noticed the anger in her eyes, but his mind was too focused to register it. Instead, he reached for the door and walked out, thinking only of how his father had threatened his family.

He jumped in his truck and drove around town until he found his father's best friend, Matt Coby. Then he bugged the shit out of the old man until he finally caved and told him where his father was staying. As he drove up to Coby's old hunting cabin, he thought of a million ways to kill his father.

Jill Sanders

Chapter Eleven

Savannah paced back and forth and felt like screaming. But she could hear Maggie playing in her crib quietly and knew she couldn't handle a crying baby at the moment.

An hour after Billy stormed out the front door, she picked up her phone and called the only person she knew could help.

When Sheriff Miller knocked on her door less than ten minutes later, she pulled him into the house and quickly told him the entire story.

Before saying anything to her, he picked up his phone and made a call.

She stood there, trying hard not to bite her nails

in frustration. She was angrier with Billy than she'd ever been. Her mind flashed to how he'd looked when she'd told him what his father had said. For the first time since she'd known him, he'd looked hard, meaner somehow. His jaw had clenched tight and a small vein had throbbed on his left temple.

Why had he let his father bully him into paying him? She'd learned a lesson early on in life. Once you let a bully in, they never stopped. Never.

She knew she didn't have any rights as far as Billy was concerned, but she thought that over the last six months they had come to understand one another. She'd felt they'd become closer, friends, at least. Why hadn't he mentioned to her that his father had gotten out of prison?

She closed her eyes and listened to the sheriff talking to Wes Tanner, one of his deputies, on the phone. When she heard the sheriff putting out an APB on Billy, her eyes flew open.

"What are you doing?" She rushed over to him. "You aren't going to arrest Billy are you?" She took his arm and tugged on it. He told Wes to hang on a minute and then held the phone away.

"Of course not. Jr. that is. Sr...." He drifted the statement off. "I guess it depends on what he's done since he's gotten out. If he hasn't checked in with his parole officer..." He started to walk out. "But my guys are looking for Billy Jr., as well. I figured he's had enough time to catch up with his old man by now." He removed his hat and shook his head. "The apple fell far from that tree." He chuckled. Then he looked off towards the back bedroom. "That little one of yours okay?" He nodded as Maggie started to cry.

"Yeah." She walked towards the back to get her and smiled when the sheriff followed her.

"You sure have turned this place into a home," he said behind her.

She glanced over her shoulder as she picked up Maggie.

"I mean"—he coughed—"of course when I lived here it was a home, but..." He shook his head and smiled as he looked at Maggie's bedroom. "Nothing like this." He chuckled.

She nodded. "Maggie seems to like frogs."

"If I remember correctly, you had a thing for rabbits when you were her age."

"Rabbits?" She frowned a little as a memory flooded back into her mind.

"Sure, I got you a little stuffed one the day..." He dropped off and when she looked at him, he looked uncomfortable.

"It's okay." She nodded. "I remember now." She smiled.

He walked over and ran the back of his fingers gently over Maggie's cheek, drying the tears that were there as she snuggled into Savannah's

151

shoulder. "I'll make sure Mr. Jackson stays clear of this place." He turned to go.

"Sheriff?" She waited until he turned around. "I never did thank you for everything you did for me. Back then." His eyes went wide, and then a slight frown formed on his lips.

"Didn't have to." He nodded and walked out of her house.

She sat down in the rocking chair and rocked Maggie as she fed her. Billy was right; Maggie's teeth were coming in and the last time she'd gone to the doctor, he'd mentioned that Maggie could start having more baby food and less breast milk.

She reached for her cell phone and tried Billy's number again. When it went to his voice mail, she hung up and closed her eyes as she leaned her head back.

She was really worried about him, about what he would do. She knew he'd protect his daughter, but she hadn't counted on seeing that much anger in his eyes when she'd told him about his father.

Her mind jumped back to her uncle. For the first time she realized just how alike she and Billy really were.

As Billy was driving back into town, he

frowned when he saw the flashing lights behind his truck. Damn, just what he needed now. A speeding ticket. He frowned when he looked down at his dash and realized he'd been going five miles under the speed limit.

Pulling over, he sighed, knowing it was Savannah's doing. He watched as Wes Tanner got out of his car and walked over to the side of his truck.

"Hey, Billy," he said, tipping his hat back and leaning against his truck.

"Hey, Wes. Did Savannah put you up to this?"

Wes nodded. "The sheriff wants me to make sure you get home safe."

Billy laughed. "No, the good sheriff wants you to make sure I don't hunt my father down and kill him for threatening my family."

Wes nodded. "That too. I'll just follow you back to your place."

"Might as well. I couldn't find the son-of-a-bitch." He frowned and felt like beating his fists against the steering wheel.

"Well, we'll do it for you. Sounds like he hasn't checked in with his parole officer this week."

"Good." Billy smiled a little. "Then he'll be going back in."

"Could be, you never know." Wes shook his head and tapped his truck. "I'll follow you back."

153

Billy nodded and waited for Wes to get back into his car, and then he drove back into town. For the first time in almost a year, he desperately wished for a beer.

When they drove up to the small house, Savannah was standing on the front porch with Maggie in her arms, looking worried. Wes honked his horn and continued to drive down the street. Billy waved at him and locked up his truck and then walked up the few steps and engulfed his two girls in his arms.

"I'm sorry," he whispered into Savannah's hair. He felt some of the tension leave her body as she relaxed against him. "I'm sorry," he repeated and placed a soft kiss on the top of her head. "Let's go inside." He glanced over his shoulder as a car drove down the street.

She nodded and stepped back from him. He could see that there was worry in her eyes instead of the anger he'd seen when he'd left the house half an hour ago.

He followed her inside and she set Maggie down in her playpen. Maggie started to fuss, but Savannah handed her a stuffed frog and the baby settled down happily, sucking on her pacifier.

He walked over and sat on the couch, feeling drained all of a sudden.

"Did you find him?" She turned to him, her arms crossing over her beautiful chest.

He shook his head no. "He's staying at Matt Coby's old hunting lease." He closed his eyes and leaned his head back. "What did the sheriff have to say?"

He heard her walk across the floor towards him. "Not much, just that they'd check to see if he was checking in with his parole officer." He opened his eyes when she sat next to him.

"He's not." When she continued to look at him, he finished. "Wes told me." She nodded. "That doesn't mean much, just that they have a reason to stop him. I'm sorry," he said again.

"For?" She looked at him blankly. "For leaving? Or for you father?"

"For my old man." He felt like slamming his fist into something, but instead closed his eyes again and rested his head back on the couch.

"Don't be." He thought he heard anger in her voice, and he opened his eyes again.

"Are you still mad at me?"

She didn't say anything for a while and then nodded slowly.

"Why? For the diner?" She shook her head no and rubbed her forehead with her fingers. "For my father?" Again, she shook her head no. "Damn it, Savvy, talk to me."

She chuckled quickly and then stood up and started pacing in front of him.

"I guess it's true what my mother always told me."

He leaned forward and rested his elbows on his knees and waited.

"Men are stupid." She chuckled again. She turned to him. "Okay, I'll spell it out for you." She held up her hand and started ticking off items on her fingers. "First, you didn't tell me that your father was out of prison." She held up her hand to stop him from interrupting. He wanted to tell her that he hadn't thought of it, but instead he leaned back and waited for her to finish. "Second, you didn't tell me that he threatened us and that you paid him off." She ticked off another finger. "Third, when I told you what happened earlier, the first thing that ran through that big, fat head of yours"—she glanced over at the playpen quickly and winced when she saw Maggie watching them closely, then changed her tone to the sweetest voice he'd ever heard —"was to chase down your father instead of staying here with us." Her eyes were glued to their daughter as she smiled at the little girl.

When her words finally sunk in, he felt a tingling sensation start in his chest and radiate throughout his entire body, causing his head to go light. "I didn't think you were in any danger. I didn't mean to just leave you two here." He felt himself stuttering and clenched his jaw.

"Of course you didn't," she said quickly. "It's

not that." She turned away from him and stared out the front living room window.

"Then what?" He stood up and walked behind her, placing his hands on her shoulder and turning her towards him.

"I just thought…" He felt her shoulders stiffen. "I thought we would solve the problem together."

He continued to look down at her, not really understanding.

"I mean, I know we haven't been…together." Color flooded her face. "But, Billy, when something like this affects us"—she glanced over his shoulder towards Maggie—"I just thought…"

It hit him. For the first time since returning home, he realized what she'd been mad at him for. Dropping his arms to his side, he felt another wave of disgust rush through him. Here he was, wanting to act like they were a family, and he was the one that had closed her out.

He realized he'd just been standing there looking down at her, so he pulled her close to him.

"I'm sorry for shutting you out. For not including you in what was going on," he said softly against her hair. "I didn't think…" He shook his head.

She pushed away and looked up at him. "That was obvious," she said as a slow smile filled her face. She was looking up at him, and he enjoyed the way the side of her mouth turned upwards. Her eyes lit up when she smiled, something he hadn't ever noticed about her before.

Who was he fooling? There was a lot about her that he hadn't noticed before. Even though he'd been infatuated with her for years, he'd never seen this side of Savannah before. Nor had he ever thought it existed.

In all the years he'd known her, she'd always been trying to stay ahead of the crowd, get something from someone, or tear someone down. Never had he seen the funny side of her. But he enjoyed it and wanted to do everything he could to see it more often.

He chuckled and then said, "I'm thinking now." He waited until she finally caught up with his mood. Her blue eyes turned warm and color flooded into her face again. Her arms wrapped around his shoulders as he pulled her hips towards his. He felt another jolt rush through his body; this time it was heat and desire.

Then he glanced over at Maggie, who was still watching them while sucking on her pacifier and hugging her stuffed frog. "Will she be okay?"

Savannah glanced over at the crib and then back up at him and nodded.

"Good, because what I have planned to make up with you…" He leaned down and placed his lips against her own soft ones. The taste of her was perfection. He couldn't explain it if he had to, but something just called him to explore her mouth even more. His fingers flexed on her hips and he wished more than anything that he could slowly slip her out of her clothes and make love to her for the rest of the day.

His fingers inched up until he felt the soft skin underneath her shirt, and then he went up farther until she was moaning against his mouth, panting with desire.

Her fingers dug into his arms and shoulders, pulling him closer, begging him for more. When he started walking her to the back of the house, the doorbell rang. Sighing, he dropped a soft kiss on her lips and closed his eyes and tried to settle his libido down.

"It's probably the sheriff." He groaned. "Damn my father for causing this mess," he said under his breath.

When he opened the door, he was shocked to see Savannah's parents standing outside, looking very worried. When they saw Savannah, they rushed in and started talking all at once, asking her a million questions, and he knew it would be a long time before Savannah and he could be alone again.

Chapter Twelve

Even though she was happy to see her parents and get a little extra attention, she desperately wished they would leave. She kept sneaking glances at Billy from across the room as her parents continued to ask her questions, and the heated glances he gave her told her that he wanted her as much as she wanted him.

Her mother had rushed in and snatched up Maggie quickly, giving as much attention as she could to the baby as her father flooded her and Billy with a million questions about what had happened.

"Why didn't we know he was getting out?"

Isn't there some sort of law saying you needed to be notified?" He frowned as he sipped his iced tea.

The three of them—Billy, her father, and herself —had retreated to the kitchen, while her mother played with Maggie in the front room. She'd poured her father a cold glass of tea and sat patiently answering all of his questions.

"No, I don't think so." Billy frowned. "I'm not the one he hurt. I'm sure the family of the man he killed was notified." He frowned again and she could tell he was remembering the fact that his father had actually killed someone at one time.

She reached across the table and took his hand. Seeing his frown turn up a little, she smiled over at him and wished she could know what was going on in his head. He squeezed her hand and answered her father's next questions, while still holding her hand in his.

When dinnertime rolled around, her father and Billy were still talking, so she pulled a pan of frozen lasagna out of the freezer and heated the oven.

Walking into the front room, she stopped and smiled as she watched her mother reading to Maggie. Maggie's little brown eyes were glued to her mother's face as she read the story in a funny voice. Leaning against the door frame, she watched the pair for a while before asking if they wanted to stay for dinner.

"Oh, of course dear." Her mother smiled and picked up Maggie. "If you need any help...?"

"No, it's just a frozen lasagna I made last week. I find it easier to make things and freeze them for nights when Maggie won't let me cook." She took her daughter from her mother. Maggie grabbed her face in her hands and started chewing on her chin.

"She's teething," her mother said. "You know, when you were teething, I used to slip a little bourbon on your gums." She smiled at her.

"I've heard of that." She frowned. Just the thought of giving her daughter something she used to drink too much of a little over a year ago made her cringe.

"I think I'll stick to the frozen rings the doctor gave me." She walked into the kitchen and pulled one of them out and gave the soft thing to Maggie, who started sucking on it. She set her in her highchair next to Billy, who helped put her little kicking legs into the right spots.

"Dad, do you want more tea?" Her father shook his head just as the doorbell rang again. When she glanced over at Billy, he got up.

"I'll get it." She watched him walk out of the room and wished more than anything to be alone with him again.

It was Lauren and her husband, stopping by to see if they could help in any way. They stayed for a little while but left when the lasagna was pulled from the oven.

Lauren hugged Savannah, and she told her she'd see her tomorrow during reading time. But after she'd closed the door, Billy took her by the shoulders and pulled her into the hallway.

"I don't think it's wise for you to go to reading time tomorrow. At least until they find my father." He frowned down at her.

She sighed. "It's less than a block away. Besides, it's in a very public place. What could go wrong?"

She crossed her arms over her chest, waiting.

"Savvy, please. I think for the next few days we should just lay low." He smiled and pulled her closer. "You know, stay at home and entertain ourselves." He spoke in a low tone so her parents wouldn't hear.

She looked up into his dark eyes and melted, thinking of all the possibilities. "I think we could keep ourselves busy for a few days." She sighed when he pulled her closer and kissed her softly.

Her parents stayed until she put Maggie down for bed. It was wonderful how much they enjoyed being around Billy. She'd never thought her father would warm up to him, but as they sat in the living room watching sports, she couldn't imagine them not getting along. They rooted for the same teams and enjoyed most of the same players.

"Men and football in Texas," her mother said,

shaking her head as she changed Maggie and got her ready for bed.

Maggie nodded. Her father had always loved the sport. At one point in her childhood, she'd thought her father was disappointed that he had a tiara-wearing daughter instead of a football-playing son.

"Mom?" She waited until her mother picked up her daughter and turned towards her. "Do you think I'm a good person?"

"Of course you are, dear." Her mother looked at her. "What brought this on?"

Savannah shook her head. "I know what people have said about me in the past." She walked over and sat in the rocking chair.

"Oh, dear, we all go through growing pains." Her mother smiled down at her as she handed Maggie to her.

"Yes, but…" She started feeding her daughter and felt her entire body relax with the comfort of the baby in her arms. "But I've said and done things that I'm ashamed of." She closed her eyes and leaned her head back.

"That's the wonderful thing about the people around here; they easily forget and forgive."

She opened her eyes and looked up at her mother and shook her head. "I don't think everyone can forget some of the things I've done."

Her mother chuckled and pulled the footstool over and sat in front of her.

"Savannah Marie Douglas, I didn't raise a fool. Sure, you had your wild times. Lord knows I have the gray hair to prove how wild you were. But all anyone would have to do is look at you now. The way you are with your daughter, the way you are with Billy." Her mother smiled. "Who would have thought that all it would take was having a good man and a beautiful daughter to turn you into the woman we always knew you'd be."

She hadn't realized she was crying until her mother leaned forward and wiped a tear from her cheek.

Her mother leaned back. "What's this all about?"

She shrugged her shoulders. "With everything that's been going on—you know, Billy's dad—it makes me wonder and remember what people have said about me in the past. I know that Uncle…" She shook her head. "Dad's brother"—she still couldn't bring herself to say his name—"was always viewed like a saint, then…"

Her mother broke in. "You may not remember, but I went to school with both Joe and your father. The two boys were as different as night and day." Her mother leaned back and shook her head. "But I never expected anything like what…" She closed her eyes and this time it was her mother's face that was wet. "I never imagined. Neither of us did.

Billy's father moved to Fairplay shortly after we graduated, and he was a few years younger than us, but I know what people said when they moved into town. They knew he was trouble, just like Joe. I think at one point they were even friends." She shook her head. "Having a bad apple in the family doesn't automatically make you bad, or mean that it will be passed down." She leaned forward and brushed a finger across Maggie's hair. "Now, don't worry about what people say or think about you anymore. I know during school you were always so competitive about everything." She smiled. "But now you have a wonderful family and a beautiful home. What's in the past is done and anyone who takes a moment to look at you would know that you've grown and changed." She smiled and patted her hand.

Savannah smiled and looked down at her daughter. "Thanks, Mom."

"Finally," Billy said, locking the door and turning to Savannah, who stood directly behind him. "Not that I don't enjoy eating dinner and watching sports with your folks, but I'm glad they're gone." He turned towards her and she took a few steps back, smiling. "Now, where were we?"

He started walking slowly towards her and

167

laughed when she darted back towards their room, laughing.

A few hours later, when he lay in bed holding Savannah, he stared up at the dark ceiling and listened to the night sounds, trying to get his mind to shut down.

He had less than a week and a half before he had to leave and head south. Being away from his family for two weeks was going to be hell. There was no way he was leaving Savannah and Maggie unless his father was back behind bars.

Savannah twitched in sleep and he pulled her closer, not wanting to let go of her soft, warm skin. He hadn't planned on falling for her, but so much had changed in the last year. He had changed. He almost chuckled out loud but caught himself for fear of waking her up. He never would have guessed a year ago that he'd be a father let alone be here with Savannah like this.

He brushed his hand over her shoulder and smiled when she moaned. She was so different than the girl he'd grown up with. She was still so very strong and beautiful, even more so now, in his opinion. But in the last year, he's seen a side of her that he never would have imagined she had. And she was really a terrific mother.

He brushed her soft hair and closed his eyes and enjoyed the feel of her next to him as he drifted off.

When he woke, it was to his daughter sitting on his chest and Savannah laughing.

"I thought you'd never wake up." She smiled, holding Maggie to keep her from falling off his chest. His arms came up and he pulled them both down on the bed as they laughed.

He buried his face into his girls and enjoyed the smell of baby powder mixed with the sexy scent of Savannah.

"Why don't you watch her while I grab a shower," Savannah said a short while later.

He nodded and stole a kiss, causing her to laugh at first, then moan and pull him closer until they were both breathless.

When she disappeared into the bathroom, he hoisted Maggie on his hip and walked into the kitchen. Setting her down in her high chair, he dumped a handful of Cheerios in front of her and watched her attack them with her little fingers.

It wasn't often that he cooked, but when he did, it was usually breakfast food. So as Savannah showered, he whipped up a batch of one of the only things he could make well: blueberry pancakes with scrambled eggs and bacon on the side.

By the time that Savannah walked into the room, looking sexy and fresh, the food was ready.

"Something smells wonderful in here." She walked in and he stopped what he was doing. She

169

was wearing a cream pair of capri pants and a silky burgundy colored shirt. She wore thin-strapped heels and her hair was curled like he always enjoyed it.

"You look amazing," he said, taking a step towards her. Then it dawned on him. She was dressed to go out. He stopped cold and crossed his arms over his chest. "I thought we talked about this."

She smiled and walked around him, taking up a plate. "Talked about what?"

"That we were going to stay put for the next few days. At least until they found my father."

She shrugged her shoulders. "If you remember, I never really agreed to that." She took two pancakes and started scooping up some scrambled eggs.

"Savvy." He took her shoulders in his hands and turned her away from the food. "I mean it. You two are staying put for the next few days."

She set her plate down and crossed her arms over her chest. "If you are so worried about it, why don't you come with us?"

He looked at her and blinked a few times. "To Mother's Reading Time?" She nodded. "Isn't it just for mothers?"

"Yes, but I'm sure that everyone will understand due to the circumstances."

He thought about it and nodded. "Fine, but I'll need a shower first."

She nodded and turned back to the food. "This does really smell wonderful." She glanced over at him and he wondered if there would ever be a time in their life when he wouldn't give her everything she ever wanted.

Chapter Thirteen

She couldn't help but laugh at Billy. He was sitting in what had to be the smallest chair in Holly's shop with Maggie on his lap, and he had a tiara strapped on his head.

There were three little girls running around him with wands, all trying to turn him into a frog. And he was being a really good sport about it all.

All of the other mothers had gathered at the bar area while the kids played in the back room. She sat at the bar and sipped her tea and watched Billy.

"So, have you heard anything?" Lauren sat next to her.

Savannah shook her head. "Nothing so far." She glanced out the large front windows and bit her bottom lip.

"Don't worry. I'm sure nothing is going to happen. After all, half the town is keeping their eyes open for him." This time it was Alex who spoke. Since they'd never really gotten along, it took Savannah by surprise. She couldn't say anything in response, so she just nodded her head. The funny thing was, she believed Alex was being one hundred percent sincere. She was even looking out the front windows, as if she were worried too.

Savannah sighed and glanced back at Billy, who was trying hard to get the kids settled down so April could start reading the chosen book for the day.

"I guess we'd better go help." She pushed her cup of tea aside and walked to the back of the room and picked up Maggie from Billy's lap.

She tried to enjoy reading time, but her mind was too occupied with everything else that was going on, and she wished that she hadn't insisted on coming along today.

When the story was over, she made some excuse and tugged on Billy's hand. They walked out the front doors less than five minutes after story time was over.

Maggie had fussed a little when she'd put her in the stroller, and so Billy had picked her up and

174

carried her instead.

"What do you say we stop off at the Grocery Stop and buy some supplies." He nodded down the street towards the only grocery store in Fairplay.

She shrugged her shoulders and followed him as he walked towards the old building.

"Haley was asking me if we had enrolled Maggie in preschool yet." He glanced over at her with a worried look. "Have we?"

She shook her head no. "Not yet. She's only seven months old." She stopped short. "That's too early, right?"

He laughed quickly and shook his head. "I don't know. I mean, I thought you knew."

She sighed and started walking again. "I guess I'll find out."

He pulled on her hand until she stopped and looked back at him. "I can find out. I was just seeing if you knew."

She nodded. "I don't mind, really." Then she laughed out loud until her sides almost hurt.

"What?" He tugged on her arm until she stopped. "What?" She stopped laughing when she saw the worry come into his eyes.

"You. Me. Us. Here." She motioned around them. "Walking to the Grocery Stop, talking about enrolling our daughter into preschool. *Our* daughter." She tried to emphasize how absurd it all was. "Did you ever imagine this?"

His eyebrows were bunched up and he was looking at her funny. So she shook her head and started to walk again.

"Wait," he said, stopping her. "No, no I never imagined anything like this. I never imagined that I'd be lucky enough to live past the age of twenty, let alone have someone like you or have a beautiful daughter, a nice home. I never imagined that you'd be with someone like me." He took a step closer to her and, with Maggie still in his arms, pulled her as close as he could. She could see emotions flood into his dark eyes and was so caught up in them, she didn't notice time or place. "I never imagined I'd be this lucky."

She couldn't stop herself. Reaching up, she took his face in her hands and pulled him down to her until their lips met. She thought she heard a whistle and a howl as someone drove by, but she didn't care. All she knew was that her heart had done a flip as he'd made his little speech. She'd never been given poetry. Never been treated as something to be cherished before. She knew part of that was her fault. She'd pushed people aside, except when she'd wanted something from them. Now, however, she wondered why she'd shielded herself for so long.

When she finally pulled away, she looked up into his eyes and smiled up at him.

"Now," she sighed, "how about we add some

Oreo ice cream to that list of yours. I feel like celebrating."

He laughed and then nodded and pulled her close again.

When they walked into the Grocery Stop, Savannah stopped cold when she saw Carmen standing behind the counter, crying. Rushing over to her, she moved behind the counter and took her friend's shoulders.

"What's wrong?"

Carmen looked up at her and wiped her nose. "He's won." She hiccuped.

"Who's won?"

"Tom, my ex. He isn't going to pay me a dime, and he's taking the kids." She burst out crying again.

"What do you mean?" Savannah shook her friend's shoulders.

Carmen wiped her tears one more time and took a deep breath. "He just called here to tell me that he's filling an appeal. Which means more money I'll have to spend on a lawyer fighting him. Which means more time away from my kids because I'll have to get another job in Tyler." She burst out crying.

"Can't you just work more hours here?" Savannah asked, patting Carmen on the shoulders.

Carmen shook her head no. "They can't afford

177

it. Besides, there are three other clerks that need the hours." She sighed. "Last time my lawyer bill was five thousand dollars. It took me a whole year to pay him back." She closed her eyes and sighed.

"Well, this is just ridiculous," Savannah said, pulling her purse out from Maggie's stroller.

"What?" Carmen started to say. "What are you doing?"

Savannah looked over at her friend. "Giving you a check so you can hire a lawyer to fight that bastard. You've worked your butt off for your money and you deserve every dime, not him." She ripped the check off and held it out for Carmen, who shook her head and put her hands behind her back.

"I...I couldn't." She looked down at the check.

Billy walked up behind them and took Savannah's arm in his. "Savvy?"

"Hush now, this is my money, and I'll do what I want with it. Besides, those two babies of yours belong in Fairplay, not in some big city, sitting home alone while their daddy runs around chasing skirts." She held the check out farther.

"Please." Carmen shook her head no.

Savannah took a step closer. "Carmen, I've known you for how long?"

Carmen swallowed and thought about it. "We were in the same kindergarten class."

Savannah smiled. "See, I didn't even know that. My point is, up until a few months ago, I didn't even give you a second thought. Then, one day, when I needed someone to talk to, you were there, no questions asked, not wanting anything from me. You listened to me ball my eyes out and have stood beside me ever since. You've become one of my closest friends. Now, if I can't give you the same help in return, then I have to question our friendship."

Carmen laughed and nodded, and then reached out for the check. "But I'm paying you back."

"Sounds fair enough. Just take your time okay?"

Carmen nodded and surprised her by grabbing onto her and giving her a huge hug.

Billy was quiet on the short walk home. The stroller was weighed down by a gallon of ice cream, several boxes of his favorite cold cereal, and a bag of cookies.

When they walked into the house, he watched her walk into the kitchen to put the ice cream away. Maggie had fallen asleep and instead of lifting her from the stroller, he let her continue to sleep comfortably in the living room.

When Savannah was done putting the frozen treats away, she turned and bumped solidly into him. He'd positioned himself just so. His hands went to her shoulders as he watched annoyance cross her blue eyes.

"This place is too small for you to sneak up on me like that," she said and he watched the heat seep into her face.

He smiled a little. "You impress me." Her jaw dropped.

"I what?" She tried to take a step back, so he followed her and moved her up against the fridge.

"You heard me," he whispered.

She shook her head and her eyes went to his lips. He smiled a little as he took another step towards her, completely pinning her to the front of the fridge. Her breath hitched as she felt his hardness against her soft stomach. Her breasts pushed up against his chest. He closed his eyes and moaned with the softness of them.

"Bill—"

He leaned down and claimed her mouth with his before she could say anything more. She tasted better than any sweets. His hands fisted, taking her shirt with him as he yanked it over her head quickly. Then he cupped those luscious tits and bent his head to have a taste. In the back of his thoughts, he heard her moan his name, but he was too far gone to notice or care how loud she was being. He pushed her bra aside and took her nipple into his mouth and enjoyed feeling her buck next to him. He pushed her leggings down her hips until he cupped her hot moist sex with his hand. When she screamed, he moved back up and took her mouth with his, muffling the sexy noises.

Her fingernails dug into his shoulders. As he pushed first one then another finger deep into her core, she ripped at his pants until they fell down by his ankles. Then she cupped him and wrapped those long fingers around his cock until he felt he'd come in her hand.

Using his thighs, he pushed her legs apart and in one quick motion, took her right there against the refrigerator. She toed off her shoes and leggings, then wrapped those long legs of hers around his hips, and he rode her hard and fast.

He felt her inner muscles clench against him and felt her body tense with her release, but he wanted more. He had to have more of her.

Running his mouth down her neck, he took her nipple deep in his mouth and sucked as he continued to pump his hips harder and faster until he felt her nails dig into his bare shoulders under his shirt.

All he could focus on were her sweet moans and how sexy she sounded, how sexy she'd look and feel laid out for him to do what he wanted. Then, when he didn't think he could hold back any more, she reached around and slapped his left butt cheek hard, causing a slight sting to spread. A burst of laughter jumped from his chest when he released deep inside her.

Resting his head against the cool fridge door, he realized that he'd just been wrecked for any other woman.

Later, after taking a quick shower and laying Maggie down in her playpen, they ate ice cream and stuffed themselves on cookies as they watched a very bad movie they'd rented.

When it was time to feed and bathe Maggie, they took a break and enjoyed the task together. He loved watching how Savannah was with their daughter. She was like a completely different person, like the one he'd seen helping that woman at the Grocery Stop.

It was funny that she'd willingly give five grand to a stranger but put her foot down when it came to paying blackmail to his father.

Just one more reason he was quickly falling deeply in love with her. Not to mention the hot kitchen sex and that sexy body of hers. He smiled as he watched her bend over and pick up one of Maggie's toys she'd tossed on the ground.

"Mmm mmm, mmm," he said, shaking his head and causing her to turn and look at him.

"What?" She frowned at him.

He laughed. "That ass of yours." He shook his head, causing her to frown more and turn to try and get a look at her butt.

"What?" she said again. This time he could hear a little more urgency in her tone.

He stood up and walked over to her, putting his arms around her. "We have got to do something about how it controls me," he said just before he took her mouth with his again.

He felt her relax a little as her arms wrapped around his shoulders. When he tried to deepen the kiss, she pulled back and shook her head.

"Oh, no. It's play time." She smiled down at Maggie, who was staring up at them with a funny look on her face.

"She's too young to know what we're doing," he said, trying to go back in for another kiss. Savannah laughed and sidestepped him.

"She may be, but I'd know. Besides, I have to do something after eating all those sweets."

He nodded and could feel all the sugar pumping through him as well. His idea of working it off and hers were completely different.

Frowning down at his daughter, he walked over and picked her up. "What do you say to another walk?" He looked over at Savannah. "Just a short one. How about around the block."

While on their evening walk around the block, he spotted the patrol car slowly following them again. He'd noticed there had been one earlier, but doubted Savannah had noticed. If she had, she hadn't mentioned it.

Knowing it was still back there assured him that they hadn't found his father yet. Something else for him to worry about. He tried not to frown as he thought about it since Savannah was watching him closely.

"I asked Carmen about preschool," she said, wrapping her arm in his.

"And?" He looked down at her.

She sighed. "We don't have to worry about it for two more years." She smiled. "Until then, Carmen and a few other mother's suggested day care." She frowned, then stopped and looked up at him. "Do you think I should get a job?"

He laughed quickly, and when he saw the anger flash in her eyes, wished he hadn't. "It's not that I don't think you can find work, it's just..." He closed his eyes and wished for a magic watch to go back to a minute ago and slap himself. "No, I don't think you should get a job. I had hoped—" He broke off when the police cruiser flipped on its lights and blared past them quickly.

Instant awareness shot through him as Maggie started crying because of the loud sound.

"Come on, let's get back to the house," he said, his eyes darting everywhere. He doubted his father was around, but he didn't want to chance it. As they made their way back to the house, his mind was whirling. Did that mean they had found him? Or had they been called away for something else?

It ate at him and when they made it back to the house, he'd totally forgotten about their earlier conversation. He watched out the front window for any sign and made sure his cell phone was tucked into his jeans.

Savannah busied herself with getting Maggie fed and dressed for bed. When she walked back out and stood next to him, he wrapped his arm around her shoulder and felt her stiffen beside him.

"If you want to work, work. I'd hoped that you'd want to stay home and be with the kids." His eyes focused as he watched the sheriff's cruiser stop in front of the house.

"Kids?" Savannah said quietly.

He turned and looked down at her. "Later," he promised and leaned down to place a kiss on her lips. "We'll talk." She nodded and he thought he saw some of the anger leave her eyes.

Walking over, he opened the front door just as the sheriff raised his hand to knock.

"Evening." He took off his hat and nodded to Savannah.

"Evening. Come on in." He motioned for the man to enter. "Any news?" he asked after the sheriff walked in.

He watched the older man nod and then shake

his head. "I hate to tell you this." He sighed. "We found Bill out by Matt Coby's lease." He shook his head. "I'm sorry, Billy, but he's dead."

Chapter Fourteen

Savannah stepped closer to Billy and wrapped her arms around his waist as the sheriff explained how Matt had found him.

"Now, we aren't ruling anything out yet, so I'll need a detailed agenda of where you've been since you last saw him." He pulled out his notepad and frowned. "Sorry about this." He looked towards her with a nod.

She walked Billy towards the couch and pushed on his shoulder until he sat down. His face had gone a little pale, so she rushed into the kitchen and grabbed him a glass of water.

187

When she handed it to him, he took a big drink and nodded to her, and then set the glass down.

"I hadn't known he was in town until Savannah told me. I found Coby and nagged him until he told me my father was staying at his lease. When I drove up there"—he shook his head and closed his eyes—"the place was empty. The front door was locked and there wasn't a vehicle. So I left, thinking he'd gone into town. I met Wes on the way back into town." He opened his eyes and ran his hands through his hair and over his face.

"When was the last time you saw him?"

He shook his head. "The day they sentenced him."

The sheriff's silver eyebrows rose. "Savannah told me you paid him some money a while back."

Billy nodded. "Wired him ten thousand."

The sheriff nodded. "But you didn't see him?"

Billy shook his head no.

"Okay." The sheriff frowned and stood up. "I'll let you know how our investigation goes."

Billy stood up quickly. "Does this mean he was murdered?"

The sheriff didn't answer him for a moment. "I'll let you know what I can, when I can."

Savannah rushed over and took his arm, stopping him from leaving. "Steve?" She looked up at him and he shook his head.

"Sorry, Savannah. I can't tell you anything more during an ongoing investigation."

"How?" she asked softly.

He sighed. "He was shot in the head."

She gasped and turned to see Billy storm out of the room, heading back towards Maggie's room.

"Thank you." She turned and leaned up and kissed the sheriff's cheek."

He nodded. "Between you and me, I don't think he had anything to do with it, but you know how it goes."

She nodded. "Thanks."

He looked towards the back and frowned. "Keep him in town for the next few days."

"He doesn't leave for work until next Tuesday. Then he'll be gone for two weeks."

"Fine. We should have more answers by then." He turned and put his hat back on and walked to his car.

Savannah locked the front door and rested her head against the cool wood for just a moment.

She knew how she'd felt her junior year after she'd heard her parents talking about her uncle and how he'd been found stabbed to death in his cell— relieved. But there had been an underlying sadness for her father, since it was his only brother.

She didn't know how Billy was going to take the news. She walked to the back and slowly opened Maggie's door just a little.

Billy was sitting in the rocking chair, holding Maggie and rocking her. Tears were streaming down his face as he looked down at his daughter.

"Billy?" She pushed the door open even more.

He looked up at her and shook his head. "I'm okay." He smiled a little. "A little relieved, I suppose." He stood up and walked over to her, then wrapped his arm around her as he held onto Maggie. "We won't have to worry about him coming around anymore," he said into her hair.

The next few days they had more visitors than she knew what to do with. For starters, the house was too small to fit everyone who came to pay their respects to Billy. Some people just stopped by to make sure everyone was all right, usually dropping off a dish of homemade food or sweets.

Gossip traveled fast in Fairplay, and she could tell that everyone already knew that the sheriff was questioning Billy. Lauren had told her that there was a rumor going around that Billy had killed his father because he'd assaulted her on the bridge. It was strange since in the past, she'd been the kind of person who had spread those kind of lies herself.

The sheriff had stopped by only one other time since that first night. He'd been dressed in his best suit and Jamella had been on his arm. Jamella had brought a huge pan of her stuffed chicken and a homemade pecan pie. They'd sat in the corner in the small room and talked to a few other people who had shown up at the same time.

When Savannah asked the sheriff some questions, he just shook his head and told her he wasn't there on official business, but rather to show his support for them during their time of loss.

Finally, the house emptied. She was in the kitchen cleaning up when she felt Billy's arms wrap around her.

"So much for date night," he whispered in her hair.

"Hmm?" She turned around after drying her hands.

"It's Friday. Remember? We were going to go into Tyler."

She nodded. "Next time." She smiled and wrapped her arms around his neck. He closed his eyes and rested his forehead against hers.

"Why does it seem like life keeps getting between us?"

She brushed her lips against his and nodded. "We'll have plenty of time."

He opened his eyes and looked down at her. "Will we?" His arms dropped as he started walking

191

back and forth in the small room. "I mean, so far we haven't committed anything to one another."

He turned and looked at her. She was speechless. He was right. He had proposed twice now, and each time she'd not only turned him down, but had gotten mad at him.

"We have a daughter together," she said, trying to ease her mind.

He laughed. "A lot of people have kids together. That doesn't mean they are committed to one another."

She leaned against the sink and rubbed her forehead. "What do you want?"

"You know what I want," he barked out, then closed his eyes and took a deep breath.

"I can't give you something I don't have," she said, feeling weary.

"What?" He stood across the small room and waited.

"I can't love," she blurted out.

He looked at her for a moment and then busted out laughing.

She stood there and wrapped her arms around herself, feeling tired and chilled.

"Of course you can. All anyone would have to do is watch you with Maggie for one minute to know that."

She shook her head and closed her eyes. "I can't love men."

She opened her eyes again when she felt his hands on her shoulders. "I don't understand."

She sighed. "I'm broken. I've been broken since I was six years old." She closed her eyes again and knew that she needed to tell him. Then he would understand and stop demanding something she couldn't give, would never give to any man. Ever.

"Savvy?" Just hearing the softness of his voice had tears rolling out of her eyes.

"I was abused," she said quickly. "When I was six, by my uncle. It lasted for a little over a year. I lost that part of me, the part I had to love a man. It's gone." She pushed away and started to walk out of the kitchen.

She made it to the living room before he spun her around and engulfed her in a hug that said more than any words ever could. She stood in her tiny living room in the small green house and held Billy as he cried for lost innocence.

"You're wrong, you know," he said later as they lay in the darkness.

"Hmmm?" she asked against his chest.

"One doesn't simply lose the ability to love." He brushed his hand down her hair, enjoying the softness of it, of her. She shook her head and he pushed back to look down at her. "It's inside there, somewhere." He brushed her hair away from her face. "And I hope to someday see it." He brushed his lips against hers, and then he deepened the kiss as he felt her soften in his arms.

Then the fierceness of his desire slammed into him and he pulled her underneath him, settling between her sweet legs. He rained kisses over every inch of her as he pulled the silk she'd come to bed in off her soft skin, inch by inch. Finally, when they lay there without any barriers, he took his time and explored every inch of her, enjoying the feel, the taste of her skin against his.

When he pushed her legs wide and explored her nether lips with his mouth, she arched up and cried out his name, pulling on his hair as he pleased her.

"More, give me more," he growled as he tongued her. He pushed a finger into her heat and lapped up her sweet cream when she screamed. When he felt her drifting back down to the mattress, he moved above her and slid slowly into her, enjoying the softness that welcomed him.

"You're wrong," he repeated. He knew that he was right as he felt her tighten up around him again, as she let herself go for him.

The next morning, he woke to pounding and turned over and pulled his pillow over his head to drown the noise out.

When the pounding stopped, he started to drift off again. Savannah walked in and sat next to him. "The sheriff's here." For a moment, he thought he'd dreamed it. Then she put her hand on his shoulder. Tossing the pillow aside, he sat up.

She was already dressed. Just the sight of her caused his mouth to water. Running his hands over his eyes, he tried to focus on something else, anything than what she'd told him last night.

If her uncle wasn't already dead, he'd have hunted him down and—

"Billy?" She shook his shoulder again, causing him to focus again.

"Yeah, I'll be right out."

She nodded and walked out, shutting the door behind her. He wanted nothing more than to fall back into the bed and sleep the day away, but instead he got up and walked into the bathroom and splashed cold water on his face.

When he looked at himself in the mirror, he frowned. His eyes were bright red and he looked a little paler than normal.

Popping two aspirin, he pulled on some clean clothes and walked out to see the sheriff standing at the oven flipping pancakes as Savannah sat at the kitchen table feeding Maggie mashed bananas.

"Morning," the sheriff said over his shoulder.

"Morning." Billy walked over and placed a kiss on Maggie's and Savannah's cheeks. "What's for breakfast, dear?" He chuckled as he walked over and stood next to the sheriff.

"Ha ha." He pulled the pan off the oven, flipped the last pancake onto the plate, and then turned towards him.

"I just thought you'd like to know that we're formally charging Albert Rothschild for your father's murder."

"Rothschild?" The name sounded familiar, but he couldn't place it. Then his blood chilled and his vision grayed a little. "Rothschild?"

The sheriff nodded. "The son of the man your father killed in that bar in Houston. Rothschild's car was seen in the area a few days before your father's murder. The kid even posted stuff on social media sites about how he was going to do it." He shook his head and crossed his arms over his chest, looking comfortable in the small space. Billy remembered that the man had lived here, in this house, for over twenty years.

"How old is he?" Savannah asked.

"Twenty two. He was just a kid when his father died. From the sound of it, he was better off without the man, but ever since, he'd become obsessed with paying your father back."

Billy shook his head. "So young. What will happen to him?"

"Well, he'll be tried. Probably be put away for a few years. You know how it goes. Life equals ten to twenty." He shook his head.

"Thank you." Savannah stood up and walked over to place a kiss on the older man's cheek. "For everything."

Billy watched the sheriff blush a little and nod. "You know, you don't have to thank me."

She smiled and nodded. After the sheriff left, they sat at the small table and ate their breakfast in silence.

"You're wrong you know," he said, causing her to look over at him, her eyebrows raised in question. "You can love a man. You love your father and…" He nodded towards the door that the sheriff had left just a few minutes earlier. "You love him." He shook his head. "Lucky bastards." He meant it to lighten the mood, but she just continued to frown at him. "Listen…" He reached for her hand.

"No." She stood up suddenly. "I…I'm sorry, I need to…" She looked around and, without another word, walked out of the kitchen. He heard the front door open and close and sighed as he looked across the table at Maggie, who just looked at him and mushed banana between her fingers and then smiled and laughed.

He chuckled. "I think your mother needs some time to think about stuff."

197

"Stuff." Maggie repeated, causing him to stop and stare at her.

"Stuff," he repeated and he was delighted when she mimicked him. Over the next hour, he tried hundreds of words and was disappointed when the only word she would say was stuff. Even the standard Mama and Dada, the usual words that developing babies picked up first, weren't in Maggie's vocabulary.

Chapter Fifteen

Savannah's head hurt. She walked at a quick pace and didn't stop until she hit the bridge. It was too early in the morning for anyone else to be out so she leaned against the railing and relaxed back.

For almost twenty years, she'd believed something about herself with no real reason. She pushed up from the railing and started pacing across the bridge as she thought about it.

First, there was Travis. She hadn't loved him. She'd enjoyed their time together, but he had only been the means to overcome her fear of men, of being touched. He'd helped by teaching her so she could become the woman she was today.

There had been other men in her life. Fewer than most people in town thought, but she couldn't deny that she'd learned something from each one of them, Billy included. She stopped cold and closed her eyes as she felt herself sway.

She didn't love him. She couldn't love him. He was Billy Jackson. Billy! She was supposed to marry a rich man, a man who could take her places. Take her out of Fairplay, Texas.

She walked over to the side of the bridge and looked down at the water. She hadn't realized she'd been crying until she watched a tear fall into the calm water below her.

Of course, she loved her father. She'd never questioned that. And she had a deep respect for the sheriff; he'd always been there in her life.

Why was Billy pushing the love card so hard? Why couldn't he just accept the fact that she wasn't going to be that for him?

They only had a few more days before he'd be gone for two weeks. Then she would have the time to clear her head and look at things in a more levelheaded way. When he was around, her mind turned foggy and tended to focus on one thing.

She shook her head and wiped her tears from her face. Taking her time to walk home, she came up with a plan of action for how to deal with him. She wasn't going to stop taking her pleasures, but that didn't mean she had to fight him on the emotional side.

With her shoulders pulled back, and her head a little clearer, she walked into the house and heard her daughter's first word.

"Stuff," Maggie said over and over again as Billy recorded it on his phone.

Savannah rushed over to her daughter. "She... she spoke?" Excitement rushed through her as she watched her daughter laugh and clap her hands, repeating the word.

Savannah hugged her and then looked over at Billy. "When did this start?"

He laughed. "Five seconds after you left." He frowned a little. "I can't get her to say anything else though."

The rest of the day was spent trying to get Maggie to say anything else. But the little girl was too determined and stubborn to even try. She would just smile and repeat the one word.

"I guess she's just like her mama." Billy laughed as they took their evening walk.

"Oh?" She glanced over at him, thankful that the day had been detoured from the conversations of that morning.

He nodded and smiled and she felt her heart skip a little at how handsome he was.

"She loves stuff." He laughed when she slapped at his shoulder playfully. Maggie repeated the word and they laughed again.

That night Savannah lay quietly in bed, pretending to be asleep.

She'd never lived with anyone before and wondered why it was so easy with Billy. He didn't leave clothes laying around, nor did he leave the toilet seat up like other men she'd been with. He helped with Maggie and, she had to be honest, she was enjoying that part a lot. Not that Maggie was a handful anymore, but she was enjoying having some more time to herself.

When Billy came to bed, she kept her eyes closed and was thankful when he turned off the light and settled down. Then he rolled over and pulled her close to him and sighed.

"Night," he said in her hair, causing goose bumps to rise all over her skin.

She nodded and sighed. It did feel good to be held. The sweet smell of his clean skin filled her senses and she closed her eyes to the desire.

"I can hear you thinking." He chuckled.

She turned towards him, running her hands over his bare chest. Enjoying the play of muscles, she continued to run her fingers over every inch of him as she looked into his dark eyes.

When her hand slipped lower, his eyes closed on a moan. Wrapping her fingers around the length of him, it was her turn to close her eyes and moan. He was impressive. The first time she'd seen him,

202

she'd wondered how he'd been so perfect.

"You're killing me," he growled as her hand stroked him slowly. Then he reached for her and she couldn't move fast enough. Pushing on his shoulders, she moved over him and straddled his hips as she flung off her clothes.

Then she was above him, positioning his cock so she could slide down it slowly. His hands gripped her hips as she moved downward and impaled herself fully. Her head rolled back as his fingers tightened on her hips, and then he was pushing and pulling her so she would move over him.

As she looked down at him, she let her body move until she felt herself building. When her release finally came, she was happy to hear him follow her just a few seconds later.

Resting her cheek against his chest, her eyes slid closed as their hearts beat rapidly in unison. She drifted off to the sound of his heartbeat and knew that she couldn't deny it any more. She'd let her guard slip for the first time in her life and it scared her too much to think about.

The next few days were busy. They had finally released his father's body, and Savannah had helped him make the arrangements for his burial.

Even though he'd spent a good portion of his life being embarrassed by the man, he couldn't deny him his last wishes. He was buried in the plot next to Billy's mother at the local cemetery just outside of town.

The simple casket had cost almost as much as his father had demanded in blackmail. Savannah must have realized that he was getting frustrated dealing with it all, because she stepped in and took over. Making the rest of the arrangements, she had even picked the flowers and the headstone out. It took two full days for everything to be completely arranged.

Now he was standing in the summer heat out in front of the local town hall in his best suit with Maggie in his arms. He greeted a few guests and friends who had shown up for the small service.

He was surprised at how many people showed up to show their support. It was nice knowing people could put what his father had done aside, even if he was still having difficulty with it. Of course, as he shut the outer doors and walked inside, he noticed that the room was only half filled.

Taking his place next to Savannah, he sat down and listened to the short sermon from the town's preacher.

The group followed the lead car out to the cemetery. Billy's hand was shaken more times than he could count.

He was thankful that Savannah's family was there and that she hadn't left his side the entire time.

When she'd walked out of the bathroom that morning in her dark skirt and blouse, he'd thought of a million things he'd rather do with her than attend his father's funeral. Her hair was tied in a bun at the nap of her neck in a sophisticated look.

With Maggie on her hip, she looked more mature than he'd ever seen her before. More respectable somehow.

He watched everyone who stopped and talked to her. She might not have known it, but in the eyes of the town, she'd changed. Now she was the woman he'd always imagined she'd be.

He found it hard not to watch her every chance he could. He knew she was struggling with her feelings for him. Finding out what she'd gone through as a child tore him apart, but he knew that someone as strong as she was could overcome. She'd done just that her entire life.

She'd taken charge of her life and was still doing so now. It wasn't as if he wanted to control her, just love her.

After they had lowered his father's casket into the ground, he sighed and glanced her way one more time as he talked with Travis.

"Savannah has planned a small get-together for later this evening." He glanced back at Travis.

"We'd love it if you guys would swing by."

Travis nodded. "Should we bring anything?"

He shook his head no. "She and her mother have been cooking the last two days. Everything is taken care of."

Travis nodded and reached for Holly's hand. Billy watched his friends walk away and sighed again, thinking about Savannah. When he glanced at her this time, she was smiling back at him as she held Maggie.

He watched her walk across the grass towards him and couldn't help but admire the way her hips swayed with each step. She'd always known how to turn a man on. When he'd arrived back home, she had seemed more intimidated around him, but as they had grown closer physically, she'd become more secure around him.

She stopped right in front of him, a huge smile on her face.

"Maggie learned another word today."

He reached over and took his daughter, a huge smile on his face. "Oh?"

"Dada," Maggie said and took his face into her hands and started kissing his chin.

Savannah laughed as he smiled. "That's my girl." He felt tears building behind his eyes, but he blinked them away and buried his face in his daughter's blonde hair.

By the time people started arriving at the house, the heat of the day had cooled to a warm eighty-seven. They had pulled out every chair they could and had folding tables set up in the backyard, where Savannah's father stood by the grill, flipping hamburgers.

He hadn't expected so many people to show up; there were more people there than had been at the service, including the sheriff and Jamella. Maggie had been whisked away by one of the West sisters earlier on. There was a large group of kids playing in Maggie's room, and he knew that she'd be watched after.

Savannah had been rushing around making sure everyone had drinks or plates. After a while, her mother had told her to sit down, since she was looking a little tired.

She took the seat next to him and sipped on a bottle of water. For the first time in almost a year, he nursed a beer. He only drank it because someone had handed it to him, and he didn't want to get up to hunt down a cold glass of ice tea instead.

"Thank you." He reached over and took Savannah's hand in his.

"For?" She tilted her head and her silver earrings sparkled in the dying light.

"For all this." He looked around and heard laughter coming from inside of the house. Shaking his head, he looked back at her. "Did you ever think we could have so many people in this place at once?"

She laughed and shook her head.

"Or that so many people would come out to show us how much they care?"

Her laughter stopped as she looked around the backyard. She shook her head.

"They're here for you," Billy told her.

She dropped his hand and stood. "I need to go check on Maggie." He let her go and watched her walk inside, looking a little lost and scared.

Savannah's father sat down next to him and sighed. "What'd you say to put that scared look on her face?"

He chuckled. "Nothing much." He shook his head. "Just that everyone was here because of her."

Her father shook his head. "A year ago she would have eaten up the attention. Now…she's changed a lot."

Billy nodded.

"We spoiled her. We had our reasons, and I doubt I'd change a thing, but I'm glad to see that she's changed."

He looked over at the man. He could see silver in his hair along his temple. There were lines on the man's forehead and near his eyes, but he still looked young. It was hard for Billy to imagine how this man had dealt with knowing his brother had destroyed his family so many years ago.

"Savvy told me what happened," he said, looking down at his beer and wishing for an iced tea instead.

When John didn't say anything, he glanced back up at him. He could see sadness in the man's eyes as he watched a group of older kids chase each other in the small yard.

"It's about time she let someone in." He took a sip of his drink and looked over at him.

"She thinks she can't ever love someone." He shook his head and watched her walk out the back door with Maggie in her arms.

"Well, that's just bull," her father said, causing him to laugh.

"On that we are in agreement."

Chapter Sixteen

It took her two whole days to get the house cleaned and back to the way it was before. There were still folding tables and chairs in the backyard that her father and Billy had to take back to the town hall.

They had more leftovers in the fridge and freezer than she knew what to do with. She'd made homemade chicken soup with the leftover chicken and had sent a pot home with her parents. She delivered two whole pies to Holly's place in hopes that she wouldn't see them sitting around the house and gain all the weight back.

She'd even delivered a whole meal's worth of food to Carmen and her two kids.

She enjoyed her hour visit, and Carmen updated her on hiring her lawyer back. She told her that he thought she had a very strong case against her ex and assured her that he wouldn't get full custody of her kids.

"Well, of course you do." Savannah smiled at the two kids playing quietly with Lego's on the floor.

"I hope so. It would kill me if I didn't get to see their funny faces every day." Carmen smiled at her two kids. "What about you? Are you and Billy going to have more kids?"

Savannah almost gasped, but then she thought about it. She'd always wanted lots of kids. She'd hated that she'd been an only child. But she still hadn't completely committed herself to their relationship. True, she couldn't imagine taking Maggie away from Billy, or—her blood turned cold—him taking Maggie from her. Shaking her head, she dismissed the thought. Billy would never do anything like that. He didn't have the meanness in him like his father had.

"We…we haven't talked about it," she told Carmen and then excused herself, telling Carmen that it was time to put Maggie down for a nap.

On the short walk back to the house, she pushed Maggie's stroller slowly and thought about the conversation. She and Billy hadn't talked about their future. Oh, sure, he'd proposed to her, twice now. But the first time had been because they'd

just found out she was pregnant. The second...
Why had he proposed the second time? She
stopped walking and thought back to that day in
the diner. What had they been talking about? She
couldn't really remember. All she remembered was
being embarrassed and upset that he'd proposed to
her at Mama's.

She started pushing the stroller again and
thought about their relationship, about their future.
About her future. What did she want? She knew
that all of the dreams that she'd had as a child were
gone and looking down at her sleeping baby, she
realized she no longer cared about the same things
that she had a year ago. What weighed heavy on
her now was the question of what next. What did
she want now?

Billy was scheduled to leave in two days and
she still didn't know how she felt about it. It was
only for two weeks this time, but things had
changed so much between them. She still wasn't
sure what to think about everything that had
happened between them.

As she walked by Holly's place, she waved in
to one of the sisters that was working behind the
tall bar counter. She like both of them, which was
funny, because they had been living in Fairplay for
a few years and Savannah would have never said
that about them over a year ago. They just didn't
run in the same circles she had.

Now she was thankful she didn't still run in

those circles. Several of her friends had moved out of town shortly after she'd found out she was pregnant. She'd heard that two of them were living in Houston, but other than that, she didn't know what they were doing. They hadn't called or texted her, and she'd forgotten about them with everything that had been going on in her own life.

She remembered how much it had stung that they'd stopped calling her, but now, she knew it had been for the best. Right after she'd found out she was pregnant, she'd tried to keep their friendships and it had been exhausting. They liked to go out dancing and drinking at least three times a week. Besides, they still smoked and she didn't want Maggie to be around anyone who smoked.

She stopped again in the middle of the sidewalk and closed her eyes, remembering the few times she'd pretended to smoke while she'd been pregnant.

Thank God the doctor had stifled any concerns she'd had about side effects. She'd been so stupid back then. Shaking her head, she started walking again and looked up to see Billy sitting on the front steps of the house, watching her.

"Deciding if you're going to come back home?" he asked when she was a few steps away from him.

"Hmm?" She parked the stroller in front of them and moved around to sit next to Billy.

He chuckled a little and nodded. "The way you kept stopping back there. It kept looking like you were trying to decide if you wanted to come back home or not. "

She shook her head. "No, I was just thinking of how stupid I used to be." She sighed and rested her elbow on her knees. "I can't believe I kept smoking for the first few weeks of pregnancy."

He looked at her and nodded. "I know what you mean." Shaking his head. "I can't believe how much I used to drink. Just that one sip of that beer the other day, and I was wanting a tall glass of tea instead."

She chuckled. "I can't believe I used to have the energy to go dancing three nights a week."

He chuckled, then sobered and took her hand. "Do you miss it?"

She thought about it for a moment. "If it means giving Maggie up, no." She smiled. "How about you?"

He shook his head. "If it means giving you two up, no." He pulled her close and kissed her softly on the lips and she felt something shift inside her. Something she'd been trying to hide her whole life.

Billy smiled at his computer screen and wished more than anything that he was back at home. He was two days into his fourteen-day shift and he missed his girls so much. He'd plastered his little sleeping area with pictures of the two of them, but it just didn't fill the emptiness or replace the feeling of holding either of them every night when he went to bed.

So far, he'd gotten along great with the rest of the crew. It was taking him a little while to adjust to living and working a few hundred feet above the water, but he thought he could get the hang of it. Luckily, it didn't sway and swing with the waves. He'd been told that it did move a little when they had high winds, but nothing major.

The work was hot and dirty and lasted a full fourteen hours each day. When he crawled into his bunk at night, he was almost too tired to chat with Savannah. Almost. He enjoyed that fact that she always dressed up nice for their Skype calls. Even Maggie was usually dressed in a dress or a cute outfit, with bows in her blonde hair.

"Has she said anything else?" he asked while keeping his eyes glued to the screen.

"No." She sighed and frowned a little. "I keep trying to teach her 'mama,' but she just won't say it."

He frowned a little. "I miss you," he said in a low voice. He knew Mark, his roommate, was asleep in the bunk below him, and he didn't want the conversation to wake him.

She nodded and then set Maggie down in her playpen. Then she came back to the computer and placed the laptop on her lap.

"I woke up this morning and reached for you." She frowned.

He smiled, knowing it was her way of saying that she'd missed him, too.

"Two weeks is a long time," he said, watching her eyes soften as she nodded. "I'd better get some sleep. Morning shift starts pretty early." He smiled.

"Billy?" She pulled the computer closer. "I miss you too," she said quickly and then hung up.

He couldn't stop smiling as he drifted off to sleep.

The next few days he learned a lot about working and living with a group of fifty grown men while trapped on a forty-story-tall building a mile away from anywhere. There was enough square footage for everyone to have their own space, but that didn't stop the tempers from flying when the job was demanding enough. Especially when lives were on the line. He'd found out quickly that there were a few employees that he had to watch his back around.

Since he'd been hired as a manager, he worked inside in the bull room most of the time. The bull room was a sixteen hundred square foot room that had more computer monitors then he'd ever seen.

His job on those days he worked inside was keeping the platform level. It was glorified babysitting; he pushed buttons that moved water in and out of long hulls causing the platform to move if needed.

He knew there were identical screens onshore and someone else sat in an office building watching the same information pop up. But he was in control of leveling and, for the most part, it was a boring job that demanded he not take his eyes from the screen the entire time he sat in the big chair.

He liked the days when he worked outside more. He'd walk the rig with a checklist and make sure everything was in working order. He liked getting his hands dirty and really enjoyed the fresh salt air.

By the end of each day, whether he'd spent it inside or out, his body would ache and his eyes were be dry. He knew that he'd have two whole weeks to rest up and spend with his family, but he couldn't help but wish that he could have a normal job in town. Something that would guarantee he could spend each day with his girls.

But it would be hard to match the amount of pay he was making He knew this was the only way to keep them in the tiny house and give his family what they needed.

Finally, the day arrived when he packed up his belongings and waited for the helicopter ride to the shore. He couldn't wait to hold his girls in his arms and as he drove out of Houston, he called Savannah.

"Hey, I'm just leaving Houston. I should be there in just under two hours."

"Good, we have a surprise for you." He could hear her laughing.

"Oh?" he said, keeping his eyes on the road.

"Yes, but I'm not telling until you get home."

He sighed and wished the speed limit was a great deal higher than seventy. "Be there as soon as I can."

"Drive safe," she said before hanging up.

Savannah was full of nerves again. Why did it seem like she couldn't get a handle on herself when it came to Billy?

The last two weeks had been fine. Just fine. Not exciting, not spectacular, nothing more than fine. She really did miss him. His smile, his laughter, the way he was with Maggie. But most of all, she missed him holding her at night. She didn't know when she'd become addicted to him, but it had happened.

Taking care of Maggie and going on her daily

219

walks just weren't as much fun anymore. The only time she did enjoy herself was when she went to visit Carmen or when they ran into Tracy on the bridge, which had started happening more often.

She'd even seen her and her parents at Mama's once when she was having lunch with Lauren and Holly. The girl had looked even smaller sitting next to her parents. She would have thought they looked like a cute family if she didn't know that the girl was being completely tortured by a group of kids at the school. She'd even considered going to her parents and talking to them at one point, but had talked herself out of it.

She'd been so busy yesterday getting the house ready for Billy's return, she and Maggie had missed their evening walk. It was strange; she'd missed Billy more in the last two weeks than she had the six months he'd been gone before.

With the house completely ready, she double-checked herself in the mirror one last time and was heading into the living room to check on Maggie, who was napping in her crib, when the doorbell rang.

She frowned as she walked towards it. Billy wouldn't ring the doorbell; he'd just walk right in.

Opening the door, she saw a smaller woman who looked very frazzled. Instantly she recognized her as Tracy's mother.

"Hello?" She noticed that the woman's face was

filled with worry.

"Hi, um, I'm Leslie Keys, Tracy's mother."

"Yes, I know, please." She motioned for her to come in.

"Oh, well. I was just wondering…" The woman shook her head and stayed on the front porch. "I was wondering if you've seen Tracy. She must have slipped out of her room early last night and hasn't been back. She's told us that she'd been hanging out with you sometimes."

Savannah nodded. "Yes, I take evening walks with my daughter and I've run into her a few times." Worry instantly filled Savannah's thoughts. "Normally we meet on the old highway bridge. Have you checked there?"

Her mother nodded her head. "It's just…" It was then that Savannah noticed the note Tracy's mother had clutched to her chest. "It's just that she left this." Tears filled her eyes as she handed over the note.

Savannah took it and read the small handwriting, silently.

If you don't like something about yourself, change.

"What does it mean?" Leslie asked.

Savannah shook her head. "I don't really know." She frowned and looked up when Billy's car parked in front of the house.

She watched him walk up the drive. The smile fell away from his mouth as soon as he saw her face.

"What's wrong?" He rushed over to her and took her shoulders.

"Tracy's missing." She handed him the note. "I think it's all my fault." She hadn't realized tears were falling down her face.

Billy read the note and turned to Leslie. "Have you called the sheriff?"

She nodded. "Last night." She looked at the note Billy was still holding. "He has everyone out looking for her, but they haven't found anything yet."

"We'll drive around and look for her," Savannah said, turning into the house to grab Maggie.

"Oh, that's…" Leslie started to say.

"If you write down your cell number, we'll text you if we find her," Billy said.

"Yes, well."

Savannah picked up Maggie as gently as she could and laid her in her carrier. Thankfully, she didn't even stir.

When she walked out front, Billy was back behind the wheel. "Where to?" he asked after she'd snapped the carrier into place.

"The old bridge."

He nodded and pulled out of the driveway.

"What does the note mean?" he asked as they headed out of town. Her eyes were glued to the streets, looking for any sign of Tracy.

She shook her head. "I don't really know. I mean, she'd told me some of the kids were making fun of her, but we never really talked about any specifics. Not really."

"She's that little brown-haired girl with braces, right?"

She nodded and said, "Yes" at the same time.

"Her mother said that her green jacket was missing."

Savannah nodded again. "She wears it on nights that it gets cool."

They pulled up to the old bridge and he stopped the car at the barriers. "You don't walk across this thing do you?" He turned to her with a frown.

"Of course I do. It's perfectly safe."

223

Jill Sanders

Chapter Seventeen

$\mathcal{B}$illy frowned at the rickety bridge. "They should have torn this down after the tornado." He got out of the car. "You stay here with Maggie." He stopped Savannah before she could get out, but she just shook her head no.

"She'll be okay, she's asleep. Besides, we'll just be a minute." She got out quickly and walked around the barriers.

"Tracy," she called over and over again.

He followed her, glancing all around. He quickly walked over and took Savannah's hand, not trusting any of the boards they walked on.

He felt a couple of them shift under his feet and instantly wished she'd go back to the car, but he knew better than ask.

"Billy." Savannah stopped and her eyes went big. "There's a board missing." She pointed a few feet away and the color left her face.

"Go back to the car and call the sheriff. My cell phone is in the console." He pushed her lightly until she moved. When she finally made it to the safety of the car, he started walking towards the broken planks.

"Tracy?" he called, getting closer to the edge so he could peek over. He couldn't see anything, so he moved closer. Feeling the rotted wood under him, he grabbed hold of the steel railing and inched his way closer. He was closer to the other side of the bridge now. That side was less steep than their side, which was a wall of stones piled on top of each other. He quickly thought about rushing down the shallow bank to check below.

When he got closer to the broken plank, he noticed a patch of green cotton hanging from a rusted nail.

"I'm going to head down the other side," he called out to Savannah, who was standing in front of the car holding the phone up to her ear. She nodded and started to walk forward.

"Stay put," he yelled. "It's not safe." She stopped and nodded again, then turned back to the car where he could hear Maggie crying. He sent up a silent prayer that his daughter was going to stop Savannah from following him.

He inched his way across the bridge and was thankful when his feet hit solid ground again. Then he rushed down the side of the hill towards the water. He went a little too fast and ended up falling backwards, scraping up his elbows and his back. His shirt flew up and gravel and dirt embedded in his exposed skin.

"Damn it." He stopped himself from falling into the water by grabbing a tree branch. Looking around, he frowned as he looked up at the hole in the bridge. If the girl had fallen through the opening, she would have landed in the water. He scanned both of the shorelines and when he saw something a little too green, he rushed down the river's edge.

Kneeling, he reached out with shaky fingers and felt the girl's neck for a pulse. She was pale, too pale. He noticed that her left leg and arm were twisted in an odd position.

She was cold to the touch and he closed his eyes and prayed that there was a pulse. Sighing, he felt a weak pulse and quickly removed his jacket to cover the girl up. He knew he shouldn't move her, but she needed to stay warm.

"Here," he called out. "I've found her. She's alive. She needs an ambulance," he called out. When he didn't hear Savannah call back, he got worried. Rushing up the riverside, he kept calling out and stopped when he finally heard her call back.

"They're on their way. Stay with her, keep her warm," she called out. He could hear the worry in her voice.

He went back to Tracy and knelt beside her. He removed his shirt, rolled it up, and placed it around her head like a cushion.
He rubbed her good arm and tried to get some warmth into her.

He didn't know how long it took for the sheriff and Wes to show up, but it seemed like forever. Each second, he imagined Tracy's temperature getting colder.

"How's she doing?" the sheriff asked as he slid down the hill towards him.

"Not so good. She's too cold. She has a broken leg and arm." He lifted his jacket and showed the sheriff.

Wes took over and started first aid. "How long you figure she's been down here?"

"Savannah said that they usually meet during their walks around six."

"Six last night?" Wes asked, not taking his eyes from the girl.

"Yeah." He frowned. "She was too busy getting ready for my return to go on a walk last night." He

228

stood back and watched other men arrive and felt like he was just in the way.

"I can go…" He started to turn back towards the bridge.

"We can use your help to get her up the hill," Wes said, handing him his shirt. He'd wrapped the girl in silver blankets and they put blocks around her broken arm and leg to keep them steady as they moved her.

It took them almost fifteen minutes to get the steel cage with the little girl inside up the side of the rocky hill. He had a few new cuts and bruises on his knees and hands when they finally made it to the top.

He was surprised to see a huge crowd standing at the top, cheering them on. Savannah rushed across to him and hugged him tightly.

"You're bleeding," she said as he wiped a tear from her eyes. He nodded and looked around, noticing that she'd moved the car to this side of the bridge. He knew it was a five-minute drive up to the new bridge and smiled down at her.

"Where's my other girl?" He looked towards the car.

"Here," Holly said, walking through the crowd. "I've got her."

"Dada," Maggie said loudly as he took her in his arms and wrapped one around Savannah.

They watched the paramedics load Tracy into the back of the ambulance, and then Savannah turned to him.

"I'd like to go down and wait until we hear something." He nodded.

As they followed the string of cars from the old bridge to the clinic downtown, he rested his head back and tried not to think of what could have happened if Savannah and Maggie had gone on the walk last night. If they had been the ones lying at the bottom of a gulch, broken.

When she stopped the car, he looked up. "Why are we home?"

She looked towards him. "I thought you'd want to clean up first. Besides, it will take a while for them to get her checked out."

He looked down at his clothes and realized he was covered in dirt and his own blood. He nodded and got out. "I'll be quick."

Less than a half hour later, they walked into the clinic. He still had rocks and dirt embedded into his skin, but at least he was wearing clean clothes and no longer had dirt in his hair.

"How is she?" Savannah asked Leslie.

"She's stable. They've set her leg and arm and she's awake." She smiled as a tear dripped down her face. "We had thought…" She broke off and shook her head. Her husband stepped forward and wrapped his arm around her shoulders.

"We'd thought she was committing suicide," he said, frowning down at his wife. "She's been so depressed the last year. We knew about the bullying, but didn't know what to do."

"I went to the school a dozen or so times, but Tracy would never tell us who was picking on her. None of the teachers knew either."

Savannah stepped forward. "Christy and Stephany." She shook her head. "I don't know their last names."

Leslie nodded. "Thank you."

"I…" Savannah started then shook her head. "I should have told you. Or gone to the school."

"It's okay," Leslie said, reaching out and taking Savannah's hand. "We'd seen a huge change in her since she started talking to you. I guess that's why we continued to let her meet you." She smiled. "She even started taking better care of herself. You know, she got that new haircut."

Savannah smiled. "She brought a magazine and asked me to help her pick it out."

"We thought…when she didn't come home, that she'd gone off…" Leslie closed her eyes and leaned against her husband.

"When I first met her, I thought she was on the bridge to do the same thing." Savannah closed her eyes. "But now." She shook her head. "I don't worry about that any more."

"It's because of you," Leslie said. "We can't thank you enough." She stepped closer and engulfed Savannah in a hug right there in the small waiting room of the clinic for everyone to see.

They sat and chatted with everyone who came into the clinic to check up on Tracy. The story was all over town and by the time the clinic doors shut for the night, everyone in Fairplay was talking about how Savannah had helped Tracy. Not to mention the story about Billy rescuing the poor girl from the side of the river.

Savannah had seen all the rocks and scratches on Billy's back and knew that he would be hurting. When they got home, she watched as he put Maggie to bed. As he shut the baby's door, she tugged on his hand and he followed her into the bathroom.

When she shut the door, he smiled and started removing his shirt, only to wince.

She ran a warm bath.

"In." She motioned to the bath.

He smiled again. "Yes, ma'am."

She laughed. "Don't think I'm going to crawl in there with you." She crossed her arms over her chest. "I need to clean all that dirt out of your back side."

He frowned and winced as she took out the antiseptic from the cabinet.

Before she knew it, he'd walked over to her and wrapped his arms around her.

"It could have been you," he said into her hair. "You and Maggie."

She shook her head, not really understanding him. He pulled back and looked down into her eyes.

"If you had gone on your walk last night. You or Maggie could have fallen through the bridge. It could have been you two down there. It would have killed me knowing that I never got to show you how much I love you."

She closed her eyes and swayed a little. Just hearing the words caused her heart to skip.

He took her shoulders in his hands. "You said something about scrubbing my back?" She knew he was trying to lighten the mood.

She chuckled and watched him undress and step into the warm tub. He hissed a little when the water hit his back.

His skin was puckered and red and several spots were dark with fresh blood.

"This may hurt." She grabbed a hand towel and the tweezers and got to work gently removing every pebble from his skin. When his skin was clear, she used a soft washcloth and cleaned his back one more time. He leaned back and closed his eyes, resting his head on the back of the tub.

"Why me?" She looked down at him until he opened his eyes.

He looked up at her in question. Then he leaned up and ran a damp hand over her face. "I guess I saw me in you." He stood up and wrapped a towel around his waist. She tried very hard not to appreciate his toned body as he pulled on a shirt and shorts. Then he walked over to her and wrapped her in his arms. "We're the same, you and I. I guess we were both running from our demons. You from your uncle, me from my father." He shook his head and then smiled a little. "Your strength, your caring. I couldn't stop myself from falling for you." He leaned down and placed a soft kiss on her lips.

"I love you, too," she said, looking into his dark eyes. "I was going to tell you over dessert." She laughed and shook her head. "I guess sometimes you just have to take it as you can get it." She reached up and took his face in her hands. "I didn't think I would ever feel this way about someone. I didn't think I could." She shook her head. "But, when I saw you carting Tracy up the hill…" She shook her head and closed her eyes quickly, then looked back up at him. "I knew. I knew I had changed enough to deserve love."

He shook his head. "You've always deserved love, and you've had mine for a while now."

She smiled. "Show me." She started to pull him closer, but he backed up a step and shook his head.

"No, there's one more thing standing in our way." He shocked her by getting down on one knee right there in the bathroom of their small green house. "Savannah Douglas, I love you. I want to raise our daughter and maybe a few more kids as a family. Will you marry me?"

She looked down at him in his cut-off shorts, white cotton t-shirt, and wet hair. He didn't have a fancy suit, or a fancy box with an expensive ring, but for the first time in her life, she realized this is what she'd dreamed of her entire life.

Smiling, she nodded her head. "Yes, Billy, I'll marry you."

Jill Sanders

Epilogue

Savannah stood at the edge of the dance floor and smiled across the room at Billy. The whole town of Fairplay had turned out for their wedding. She'd been extra happy that Tracy could stand as her only bridesmaid. Even though she had to lean on crutches, the young girl had smiled the entire time. Holly had shown up early at the church and had done Tracy's hair and makeup. Savannah had to admit, she looked completely beautiful and happy in her silver bridesmaid's dress.

Every seat in the large church downtown was full, and there had even been a group of people who stood along the back walls.

Everyone had laughed when Maggie had interrupted their kiss with, "Daddy kiss mommy."

Now, as she waited for the last dance at their reception in the town hall, she glanced over at her mother and father, who were going to be babysitting Maggie for the next week. She didn't know where Billy was taking her for their honeymoon, since he'd decided it was going to be a surprise. She didn't care where they went, as long as they went together.

"Ready to leave, Mrs. Jackson?" He smiled at her.

"Only if you are, husband." She smiled when he pulled her close and kissed her right on the dance floor as they swayed to the soft music. Cheers erupted, causing them to pull away and laugh.

"I say there's no time like the present." He took her hand and made a dash for the exit. But everyone was prepared and bombarded them with rice as they dashed out. She was a little breathless when they finally made it to the car.

"Who knew that Holly could run so fast." She laughed as she looked out the back of the car.

"And Tracy, even with those crutches." He smiled.

Billy had left the top down on his convertible and so they had continued to be pummeled as they drove away. Holly jogged beside the car and continued to throw rice at them until they made it out of the parking lot.

He chuckled and shook his head as he watched Holly. "Travis has been working out with her."

She laughed. "I guess it's a good thing I ended up with you." She wrapped a lock of his dark hair around her fingertip.

"Oh?" He glanced over at her.

She nodded. "Yeah, I like slow walks and…" — she leaned and whispered in his ear—"fast sex."

He blinked a few times and then, just on the outskirts of town, pulled the car over into an empty parking lot.

She took this opportunity to hike up her skirt

and move over to straddle him.

"You're killing me here." He looked around the parking lot.

"Everyone in town is still enjoying the free bar and food at the party," she whispered into his ear, pulling his face to hers. Then she took his hands and put them on her hips as she started to move over him. "Hang on to me." She smiled down at him, a wicked sparkle in her blue eyes. "This is going to be a wild ride."

Other books by Jill Sanders

The Pride Series
Finding Pride – Pride Series #1
Discovering Pride – Pride Series #2
Returning Pride – Pride Series #3
Lasting Pride – Pride Series #4
Serving Pride – Prequel to Pride Series #5
Red Hot Christmas – A Pride Christmas #6
My Sweet Valentine – Pride Series #7
Summer Crush – Pride Series #8

The Secret Series
Secret Seduction – Secret Series #1
Secret Pleasure – Secret Series #2
Secret Guardian – Secret Series #3
Secret Passions – Secret Series #4
Secret Identity – Secret Series #5
Secret Sauce – Secret Series #6

The West Series
Loving Lauren – West Series #1
Taming Alex – West Series #2
Holding Haley – West Series #3
Missy's Moment – West Series #4
Breaking Travis - West Series #5
Roping Ryan - West Series #6
Wild Bride – West Series #7

For a complete list of books, visit JillSanders.com

This is a work of fiction. Names, characters, places, and incidents are either the product of the author's imagination or are used fictitiously, and any resemblance to actual persons, living or dead, business establishments, events, or locales is entirely coincidental.

Follow Jill Sanders online at:
Web: www.jillsanders.com
Twitter: @jillmsanders
Facebook: jillsandersbooks

ISBN: 978-1503041110
Copyright © 2014 Jill Sanders
Copyeditor: Erica Ellis – inkdeepediting.com

About the Author

Jill Sanders is the New York Times and USA Today bestselling author of the Pride Series, the Secret Series, and the West Series romance novels. Having sold over 150,000 books within six months of her first release, she continues to lure new readers with her sweet and sexy stories. Her books are available in every English-speaking country, available in audio books, and are now being translated into six different languages.

Born as an identical twin in a large family, she was raised in the Pacific Northwest. She later relocated to Colorado for college and a successful IT career before discovering her talent as a writer. She now makes her home in charming rural Florida where she enjoys the beach, swimming, hiking, wine tasting, and, of course, writing.

17239340R00137

Made in the USA
Middletown, DE
13 January 2015